Glory Goes and Gets Some

Emily Carter

glory goes and gets some

stories

COFFEE HOUSE PRESS

COFFEE HOUSE PRESS is an independent nonprofit literary publisher supported in part by a grant provided by the Minnesota State Arts Board, through an appropriation by the Minnesota State Legislature, and in part by a grant from the National Endowment for the Arts. Significant support has also been provided by the Bush Foundation; Elmer L. & Eleanor J. Andersen Foundation; General Mills Foundation; Honeywell Foundation; James R. Thorpe Foundation; Lila Wallace Reader's Digest Fund; Pentair, Inc.; McKnight Foundation; Patrick and Aimee Butler Family Foundation; The St. Paul Companies Foundation, Inc.; the law firm of Schwegman, Lundberg, Woessner & Kluth, P.A.; Star Tribune Foundation; the Target Foundation; West Group; and many individual donors. To you and our many readers across the country, we send our thanks for your continuing support.

COFFEE HOUSE PRESS books are available to the trade through our primary distributor, Consortium Book Sales & Distribution, 1045 Westgate Drive, Saint Paul, MN 55114. For personal orders, catalogs, or other information, write to: Coffee House Press, 27 North Fourth Street, Suite 400, Minneapolis, MN 55401.

LIBRARY OF CONGRESS CATALOGING-IN-PUBLICATION INFORMATION
Carter, Emily, 1960–
     Glory goes and gets some : stories / by Emily Carter.
          p. cm.
     ISBN 1-56689-101-9 (alk. paper)
          I. Young women—Drug use—Fiction. 2. Narcotic
addicts—Rehabilitation—Fiction. 3. HIV-positive women—Fiction. 4.
York (N.Y.)—Fiction. 5. Minnesota—Fiction. I Title.
     PS3553.A776 G58 2000
     811'.6—DC21   00-04302

10 9 8 7 6 5 4 3 2 1
FIRST EDITION / FIRST PRINTING

PRINTED IN CANADA

For my parents,
Anne and Herman Roiphe

The author wishes to thank Bruce Cheney for years of patience and support and Johnnie Ammentorp for his sage counsel. Generous support has been provided through a Loft/McKnight Award and a Bush Foundation fellowship.

CONTENTS

1

East on Houston 15
Glory B. and the Gentle Art 19
Glory B. and the Baby Jesus 27
Glory B. and the Ice-Man 35
Glory and the Angels 43

2

Minneapolis 53
New in North Town 57
Ask Amelio 61

3

WLUV 69
Parachute Silk 81
My Big Red Heart 99

4

Luminous Dial 105
The Bride 109

5

Bad Boy Walking 145
All the Men Are Called McCabe 165
Zemecki's Cat 173

6

Cute in Camouflage 195
Glory Goes and Gets Some 207
Train Line 213
A 225
Clean Clothes 237

The city was full of lonesome monsters
who couldn't get drunk anymore.

—Nelson Algren

There was this one summer that began in June and ended quite some time later, when I could hear the voices of men in traffic, while I was walking east on Houston. They honked and squealed, barked, drawled, groaned, purred, hissed, whispered, and raggedly begged at me as I twitched down the street in a borrowed dress that was as red as the stoplights, the stoplights gleaming in the black air like costume jewelry from a sunken Spanish galleon, gleaming from the bottom of the sea: the night on Houston like a black tropical shipwreck ocean, fathoms deep and full of trinkets for a young girl like yours-ever-true.

Their voices glittered like tossed beer cans on traffic islands and said, Excuse me Miss, excuse me, can I walk you? Excuse me, excuse me Miss, those are some fine young thighs you're sliding along on there, with that creamy swish-swish, sweet, like my wife's when she was still walking. If I call her collect this one last—I'm going to tell her this time that I really mean it, this time, she'll forget about all the hours that piled up like stale blankets until she couldn't get out of bed, and we'll go to that place in Sheepshead, we'll go to that place

that serves that crab with the butter sauce you could just about make love to, and you've got those exact same thighs, Miss, just slow them down a little because I'll tell you what, you haven't seen anything yet.

Their voices reflected me in pieces of what they saw, like shattered Christmas ornaments on the sand in July: Excuse me Miss. You can stop can't you, you can spare one second, can't you? Can't you, you little cunt? You little stuck-up cunt? Think it's made of gold or what? All you cunts—don't even care what it was a man used to do for you, it's all what can you do for me right now. From watching too much television, that right-now thing—you've even got it in your walk, you walk like "right-now, right-now" . . . you don't care, do you, what I used . . . I used to . . . I used to know the first four hundred pages of the *Iliad* by heart, memorized, I could quote it from memory, fine, fine, keep walkin', you ugly at any rate.

Do I remember what it was exactly I was walking into when I was walking east on that particular street? Nothing good, but listen, the voices of men lifted me like a murmuring tide and floated me down toward the river, me with my eyeliner making my eyes black and green, smeared, shaped like tears, like black and green chalk-drawing eyes running in the rain.

I was moist, like the sky before a shower, and the voices of men clamored to me like a summer thunderstorm—Excuse me Miss, they cracked, they lit up the sky, Excuse me Miss, but I'm a jazz musician. They blew around me like a light breeze. Excuse me Miss, but do you know how to get to that little place on the end of First and A? What I mean is, I feel

a little awkward in this neighborhood, and I'd like to bring something back to show my friends, something I could give a bath and brush its hair, something to lick like a sweet poison plum, something that would climb out my fire escape in the morning and never ask to see my bank statement—I heard them say things like that. Excuse me Miss, but I'm a jazz musician. I heard them clacking their knees together, heard them say, Excuse me Miss, I'm tired and I'm no longer a young stud by any means, but if I could touch the hollow of your ankle, if I could just once see it filled with rainwater, I'd smile like a wolf and bring you something wrestled from the concrete with my bare hands, my hands stained yellow with cigarettes and strength—hell, I'd wrestle the lights off the Chrysler building if you'd just let me look at it, even though I have no teeth.

And that guy, who was always there, with his broken instrument: Excuse me Miss, but I'm a jazz, excuse me, excuse me Miss, but I used to play with Parker, Miss, excuse me, but I'm a jazz musician, and I'm talking to you . . . I heard them say it, their voices twining around, through the pointed scrawny leaves of the plane trees, around the twigs and paper cups at my feet: Excuse me Miss, but my mother was a knife-sharp, slender blue dragon, she spat white hot fire from her eyes, like lasers, and her teeth were shaped like needles, twelve feet long, her scales like sapphires; when she flew overhead she cast a shadow across the face of the sun, her talons were made of black steel, and she would have called you a bitch because you won't talk to me, Miss.

It seems to me now like I had been on roller skates, young enough to slide in and out of traffic, in between taxis and trucks. But I knew what I was walking into, and what I was listening for all along, and how after I heard it I couldn't hear much of anything else for a long time. I don't want to go back there. I only ever think about it when I hear the sound of screeching brakes.

GLORY B. AND THE GENTLE ART

All right, maybe I do. Maybe I do talk first and think later. Yes, it's true, I admit it freely. It's because I'm from the city. Now, you can say to me, Glory B., it's no crime to think about what you're going to say before you say it, to figure out how it relates to the topic being discussed, or if it does at all, or if what you're going to say has the slightest factual basis whatsoever. I've got that argument down cold, because listen, words are my music. When I talk, I improvise. It's not so much what I'm saying as how it sounds. Take jazz, all right, let's use jazz as an analogy, parallels are always good. Now, what I mean is, what—do you think every time Bird sat down to blow he had the whole musical score right in front of him? Did he have the whole thing thought out? He did not. Well, he probably did not, I'm not entirely familiar with the man's work, but probably, most likely he improvised is what I'm saying.

Now some people, people from Someplace, say, like Minnesota, they think about what they're going to say before they say it. They're not attuned to the sound of words, because they probably grew up sitting on their porches after dinner and

homework, listening to crickets, which just make one sound, over and over again, and put you in a trance so you can just sit there not moving and think, think, think, until you go inside and watch television or make fruit jellies. That's where all those types with the masters in philosophy come from: Minnesota, Wisconsin, North Dakota, like that. Brooding and musing all the time. Very, very Swedish, if you catch my drift. Trust them, why should I?

Never go to the movies with someone from Minnesota. Here's what I mean:

I have this friend, we used to go out in high school, about six hundred years ago, but he went to college and grad school while I kept forgetting to get up in the morning, and now he's my friend and he lives in Inwood, which is way far north, where the subway stations have elevators in them to get you back up to street level because you're so far underground, and when you come up you're on top of a hill and all around you is miles and miles of nothing that looks like the city you grew up in, wide boulevards with vague glittering lights from fast-food restaurants and body shops. So you see what I mean— my friend has chosen an untrendy existence in an unfashion-able part of town. So when he calls me up to tell me he has fallen in love with this amazing girl who's not only beautiful, but also brilliant, where does she come from? Well, a hint, it's a lot farther west than Fort Lee, New Jersey, and there's plenty of wheat out there. And what's she doing here? Getting her degree in Kierkegaard, another Nordic good-time boy. He tells me her name is Lara Kjellaan and he wants me to meet her, for some reason he thinks it's very important that we

meet. So all right, they'll come down from the north pole and we'll go to the movies.

When I meet them outside the theater and we all shake hands I'm thinking that I probably really am an alcoholic because one of the questions they ask you is "when you're in social situations where alcohol is not present, do you feel uncomfortable?" Answer: Yes, absolutely. Let's face it, the only thing I like to do is sit around a bar and drink alcoholic beverages. This meeting people I don't know, this going to the movies, it's not for me, really it's not. But I shake this Lara person's hand and smile warmly at her, a smile that communicates nothing so much as the fact that I have no plans to try to sleep with her boyfriend, because if we don't start from there, forget it, I won't be able to hack this evening at all, and I'm already wishing that I could just spend my whole life talking to strangers who love the sound of my voice, buy me shots of the local spirits, some kind of potent potato liquor brewed in the mountains by peasant women who mix it all up with their saliva. What's so bad about people's saliva? I think we should all share each other's saliva, why not? Saliva, of course, is something I'm thinking a lot about when I meet my old friend and his new girl, because she's very small, has sparrow-boned shoulders and ivory fingers delicate as a tree frog's knobbly feet. Her hair is the color of straw and her face is washed with a faint dusting of freckles. The whole deal makes me nervous, and when I'm nervous I tend to spit when I talk. Not much, just a little, a little mist.

When I calm down enough to hear what's going on around me I hear my friend reeling off a list of Lara's academic credits— University X, Foundation grant Y—because he thinks given

half a chance I will dismiss this sweetie as a generic love interest, which really isn't giving me any credit at all. We're all
standing in this long line and just as he gets to the part about
applying to some writer's colony the line starts to move. I hover
over Lara, ready to confide, this must be awkward for her, too?
She's hardly had the chance to say one single word, what with
her boyfriend doing her advance PR work. I remember in high
school we almost never got around, me and this guy, to making out, because he talked so much, and half the time we'd end
up in an argument about who was the biggest hypocrite and
not speak to each other for a week. We broke up by midterms,
if I remember correctly.

So I'm hovering over this Lara, and like always with really
small women, I feel like Alice after she took the one pill that
makes you larger, big and—here's the word—galumphing.
Galumphing, good word, and that of course makes me feel
this heady sensation of protectiveness toward the smaller
woman, and then the usual realization dawns on me. Oh My
God I Am A Lesbian. And not one of those hip stylish ones
who write avant-garde movie scripts and get their pictures
taken in nightclubs either. I'm some sad old thing sitting at
the bar while my little femme fatale girlfriend cheats on me
with anything, male or female, that happens to be around. In
other words, I get treated the way I've treated certain men in
my life, which as a thought is worse than thinking about car
accidents. So I say to Lara, would she like some popcorn, my
treat. She's so short I want to put my hand on her shoulder,
but I don't. I put it instead into my pocket to dig out the
money. My friend comes out of the men's room and we go

inside the theater. Then there's the thing about who sits where, which I can't stand either; it's more of that kind of thing that makes me pull at my hair when I'm sober. We could sit with my friend between us, but I don't like the looks of that—like he's got two girls, one on either side, nudge, nudge, lucky dog, heh-heh. But then again if I sit on the outside of Lara, it will look like I'm some sort of third wheel, some kind of duenna, or some horrible thing like that. I'm standing in the aisle, thinking about what it would be like to be someplace else, sitting in my kitchen for instance, or watching my insane and sorrowful upstairs neighbor Katasha write down lists of her enemies, when here comes the thought, to my rescue, like Superman. Just sit, Gloria, it doesn't matter where, because No One Is Looking At You. Hard to believe, and yet it's an ontological starting point I must adhere to, at times, even just to get out of my apartment.

Anyway, I forget about all that noise as soon as the movie starts. Let me tell you about this movie. It was amazing, and it made me cry at the end, not the kind of crying where they trick you into it with violet colored lights and a certain kind of music that attaches itself directly to your tear ducts and pulls at them like an invisible, milking jellyfish, so you feel a little ashamed of yourself for being so easily run through the maze to get your money's worth; but the kind of crying where you've just gotten a sense of the fact that there is life, and people go through it, and they die, some of them kill each other, but a man who knew nothing, not even how to talk to people, was somehow able to learn to make things grow out of the earth. Something like that.

The movie put me in a wrestling hold of excitement. Whenever I see something like that every single tendon in my arms and legs seems to buzz a little, and I feel like twitching and jumping. What this is, really, is the desire to do something like that, make that picture, paint that painting, walk that walk, talk that talk. I want to do something like that, something good. What I do when I feel like that, usually, is kill that energy as soon as possible. I go have a drink, or I eat an entire Philadelphia cheesecake, which will make it impossible to think about anything but my intestines for the next three hours. But now I've got to go for coffee, coffee of all things, and I'm walking fast, turning around every now and then to the couple behind me, saying, "Incredible. It was incredible. Fuck." My friend agrees with me. "Incredible," he echoes, but when we get to the coffee shop it turns out he's got reservations, he thinks the filmmaker could have gone further with the atrocities depicted in the war scene.

"What," I say, "the depicted atrocities weren't enough for you? You can't stand it when anyone does anything well, is what your problem is."

"I'm not saying he didn't make a good movie," my friend says, "I'm just saying that when push came to shove, he sold out." When my friend says "sold out" he bangs his fist down on the table and the coffee sloshes over his cup, running thinly over the formica and down the ridged metal edge of the table, dropping off in little beads. He doesn't notice. Lara sops it up with a napkin. Meanwhile I'm saying, "Yeah, sold out? Sold out to who? Is this man going to become rich off this film? No, I think not. Who did he sell out to then? Who?" I raise my hands in

question and knock over a bowl of sugar. I make a plow out of my hand and wipe the sugar to the floor. There are principles here, and I mean every word I'm saying. We keep going. The waitress asks us to lower our voices. Cigarette butts pile up in the ashtray. I compare the narrowness of his righteous unbending rigid thinking to that of Mussolini. He compares all my old boyfriends to Hitler. I draw an analogy between the alchemy of the movie and something about Madame Curie. Which brings up radiation, which brings up Hiroshima, and the ashtray clatters to the floor spilling gray dust and cigarettes everywhere. We work quickly to get it all up before the waitress sees it, and we continue through the Kennedy assassination, the Vietnam War, various pop stars compared to the blues singers they ripped off their music from. And finally, finally my rudeness dawns on me like a wet gray November morning. I pull in my gesturing hands which are leaping about like struggling swordfish on a tight line. I narrow the big opening my mouth makes in my face and look at Lara who has been sitting quietly through the whole discussion, looking pleasantly first at one of us, then at the other.

"Well," I say, "what about you, what do you think?" Lara takes a moment to answer. She takes so many seconds to answer that I am about to throw another question at her, because I just can't wait, I'm jumping out of my seat; but before I can, Lara says, "Well." She says, "well," and slowly, slowly, clears her throat.

"The thing about the scene you were talking about," she says and gives a little apologetic smile, "is it was about the First World War, not the Second."

The First World War. Not the Second. It's like hitting a wall of air. If this movie is about the First World War and not the Second, everything we've been saying is either completely beside the point, or ludicrously wrong. For a moment there is actually no sound at all at our table.

"Did you know that the whole time?" I ask.

"Well," she says, "yes, pretty much."

"Why didn't you stop us?"

She looks absolutely frank and undisturbed as she says, "What you were saying was interesting."

I just sit there, my arguments and brilliant parallels drifting down around me like invisible balloons with the air let out. Those people from the Midwest. Oh, they're clever. Watch the snowflakes fall, observe the sky change from blue to black to blue again, and think and think and think before they speak.

You can't trust them, you just can't. But what if she hadn't been there, what if we had gone on all night calling something that was obviously blue red—eighteen different shades of red.

"Listen," I say to my friend, "I'm not kidding, marry this woman."

GLORY B. AND THE BABY JESUS

I could never get Ex-Sister Jacqueline to tell me where she'd hidden the baby Jesus. Ex-Sister Jacqueline of Pitt Street, plump white woman with hair-sprayed blonde hair and round, quiet brown eyes. The first time I saw her, I was looking up from my doorway, which was really her doorway. I had had one of those nights when it really seems like too much effort to get to your door, fumble for your keys, stick them in the lock, and open. So I just sat down in the doorway. Except it was also one of those nights when you get your doorway confused with the doorway of the apartment one flight down which looks exactly like your doorway. Ex-Sister Jacqueline looked through her peephole and saw me crumpled at the foot of her door. Actually, she says, she could only see one foot, lying there like a fish. I was wearing mangy suede high heels. Ex-Sister Jacqueline told me she'd always wanted to wear high heels but didn't think she had the ankles for them, so she'd opened the door and looked down at me with her gentle saint-colored brown eyes. Run, I said to myself, it's a social worker. This was because of her taste in clothes, which was the worst I'd ever seen. She patiently explained to me that this was not

my apartment, but hers, and if I wasn't on crack, I could come in and have some peppermint tea, which, she said, was good for stomach or nervous-system related distress.

I'd been right about one thing, she was a social worker. But I forgave her for that once I heard her story. It could have been, as far as she was concerned, a great deal worse.

The second time I went over to her kitchen I realized there was more to Miss Ex-Sister Jackie than met the eye. We were talking about what people were usually talking about that summer: the gentrification of the neighborhood, meaning eccentrics out, young people out, people who want to pay $1500 a month for a studio apartment in. Gentle Jacqueline, a forty-year-old woman in beige polyester slacks and a checkered shirt, looked down into the tea she was stirring and said, "I'd like to strangle them all in their beds." The slight start I gave at this statement was nothing compared to my astonishment when she added, "God forgive me." I did a double take, a little nervous to realize she wasn't just talking out of the side of her mouth. She really did want to murder them all in their beds and she really did want God to forgive her for wanting to do this.

Sister Jacqueline joined the Sisters of Patience when she was seventeen years old, about a month after her father's funeral. Her father was not exactly an educated man, but drunk as he usually was, he had a kind of sixth sense when it came to his daughters. Somehow he knew when each one of them hit puberty and it was time to start beating on them.

Jacqueline's nine sisters had all jumped ship and gotten married as soon as possible. This didn't seem possible for Jackie,

however, due to the beating she received two months before her father checked out. He hit her with a tire iron when she came home late from an evening out with the lifeguard from the local community pool. He wouldn't have beat her for as long as he did, she said, but she bit her tongue to keep from making any noise. She told the doctor in the emergency room she'd fallen through the basement trapdoor. He told her that was a heck of a fall, and that she would not be able to bear any children.

After her father's funeral, her mother, perhaps taking an overview of sorts, told her to consider it a blessing. All men, her mother said, were basically variations of the same one. There was only one husband who would treat her with the respect she deserved, who would cherish her, who would keep her honor shining bright like a blue flame.

Most of the Sisters of Patience of Baltimore were delighted with her from the start. She was a perfect candidate, never uttering a peep during the year of silence that was part of the initiation imposed on the novices. Very few before her had actually not said a word for an entire year. The nuns tended to be lenient with that particular requirement, not being sure in their hearts that God had meant for seventeen-year-old girls to spend a year without speaking at all. Young Sister Jacqueline, however, had no problem with it. The other Sisters thought it was a sign of devotion. Mother Superior, however, told her that it proved only her stubbornness and the sin of pride. "You're biting your tongue," she told Sister Jacqueline. "It's cheating if you bite your tongue."

So the years go by and Sister Jacqueline becomes a working nun. She works in the community with drug addicts,

schizophrenics, prostitutes: the usual children of God. They say she is very good at it and she wins a lot of community certificates for her service. The convent takes the vow of poverty very seriously; ten dollars a week is what they live on. They are to be home every day at five-thirty. This presents a problem for Sister Jacqueline, who's inherited from her father an obsession with alcohol. Her circumstances dictate, of course, that this obsession remain a big secret. Well, here's a woman who did not talk for 365 days, can she keep a secret? The problems are logistical at first. On ten dollars a week, where will she get the money? Having to be home at five-thirty every day, how will she be able to appear sober for the evening meal? She cements her quiet, meditative, spiritual front. She pilfers money from the necessities box. She works harder, gets up earlier, stays up later than anyone else; she always smells like eucalyptus cough drops. She is not confronted because no one gets very close to her. She doesn't have many friends in the convent. She doesn't because deep down at the very bottom of her vodka bottle she has a black stubborn thought that she knows is hideous, but which she can't let go of: Nuns, she thinks, are stupid.

As the days go on, she develops a routine. She finishes a bottle and puts it under her bed until she can throw it away unobserved. The bottles pile up. She drinks about a quart of vodka daily and throws the bottles out on Monday nights, when it's her turn to do the garbage. During the brief times when she is sober, she prays: Show me what to do, give me a sign.

Then it's Sister Jacqueline's eighteenth Christmas with the Sisters of Patience and it's finally her turn to put the baby Jesus,

made out of the finest Dresden china, in the little porcelain manger. Even though the nuns take their vow of poverty very seriously they do have these Dresden china figurines for the crèche. All year long they are kept in a special blue velvet box in the chapel, wrapped in cheesecloth. A few days before Christmas they start putting them out, one by one; first the little lambs, then the cows and pigs, then the shepherds, the wisemen, then Joseph, then Mary. Finally, on Christmas Eve, Mother Superior goes over to the blue velvet box, opens it slowly, and gently unwraps the baby Jesus. She makes a little speech and hands him over to the nun who has best exemplified the tenets of poverty, chastity, and obedience, to the nun who has been the most selfless in her devotion, who has brought home the most community service awards to the convent.

That year it was Sister Jacqueline who was the most worthy. All the Sisters congratulate her on getting to place the baby Jesus in the manger. The night before Christmas Eve, Sister Jacqueline is alone in her room thinking and, of course, drinking. Eighteen years, she thinks, and she gets the big honor of putting a little doll into its stupid bed. This sets a voice clanging in her head like a bell—*mistake, mistake,* the voice peals, *your whole life has been a mistake.* A mistake. She would like to pray, but she never prays when she's drunk. Tomorrow, she thinks, I'll be downstairs in the chapel. She imagines Mother Superior handing her the little china Jesus to put in the little porcelain manger. The nuns' faces will be goofy with delight at their Sister's big achievement. Watching, they'll beam at her as she gently places the little china doll in its little porcelain bed. Porcelain, how delicate. For trinkets and toilets.

Sister Jacqueline has never used profanity of any kind, although plenty of nuns do, it's just not in her nature, but now a foul word comes jumping out of her throat like a toad. "Shit," she says, through gritted teeth into her pillow, "that is the *stupidest.*"

Late that night she creeps down into the chapel, wearing only her nightgown and socks, like a kid trying to sneak up on Santa Claus.

The next evening, sitting in the front pew of the chapel, she is drunk as usual, but silent with her eucalyptus breath, she passes for sober. The candles are lit. It's the big moment. Mother Superior says a few words about Sister Jacqueline's eighteen years of service and devotion, how she is respected and loved by the community, and then goes over to the blue velvet box. She lifts the lid slowly, teasing the nuns with the anticipation. The chapel is silent except for the hinges of the box slowly creaking. The Sisters can barely keep from craning their necks and jostling each other in the ribs. But instead of the doll coming out of the box a dove-like cry of alarm flutters from the throat of Mother Superior. The baby Jesus is missing. Distraught nuns trot around in little circles. The chapel fills with the sound of perplexed nuns, their habits swishing as they bend down, looking frantically, without much hope, under pews and behind the tabernacle. But Sister Jacqueline just sits there, swaying slightly, her brown eyes brimming. Mother Superior's glance snags her like a hook into a fish. She walks over and hisses right into her face, "Devil! You're sauced to the gills! Where have you hidden him?"

Sauced-to-the-gills Sister Jacqueline leans over into the white-hot orb of Mother Superior's face and, exhaling a gentle

breeze of eucalyptus vapor, says, "Kidnapped. Kidnapped by Satan. Oh no, sound the alarm."

And then she sinks to the floor of the chapel, passed out as cold as the marble blocks onto which she falls.

When she comes to, the nuns are gathered around her bed. She knows by their faces that they have searched her room thoroughly, that they have not found the baby Jesus, but instead they have found thirty empty vodka bottles and two full ones. They look down at her with expressions of infinite, gentle suffering. Sister Jacqueline has an urge to vomit, but nothing they say can make her tell where she has hidden the doll. She knows she is a stubborn, sinful nun, and she knows that God will never, never forgive her, but still she won't tell them. It's the only thing, that little kernel of blind will, that little thought of *get another damn doll,* that keeps her from wanting to kill herself and be lost forever.

She doesn't tell them even when they take her to the doctor who examines her and says that her blood pressure is high, her liver is distended, and she has ulcers in her throat that could open up at any time, drowning her in her own blood. Which was, Sister Jacqueline was sure, no better than she deserved.

So the nuns called on the diocese and the diocese sent Sister Jacqueline to rehab.

I asked Sister Jacqueline what went on in a rehab center. Did they brainwash her or what? "Well," she said, "for the first two months I was there, I kept my eyes pretty much on the ground. Then something strange happened." "Oh," I said, *"then* something strange happened." "I decided that I was a good person,"

she said, "but not such a good nun." "Ah ha," I said, "that's how you got here, isn't it?" "More or less," she said, giggling. At any rate, she didn't go back to the Sisters of Patience in Baltimore. She came to New York and got a job with the Catholic Relief Service. Which is what she does best, sitting with the schizos, crack addicts, and prostitutes, showing them how to fill out forms. She doesn't ask if what she's doing will change anything. "My job," Ex-Sister Jacqueline says, "is to show them how to fill out the forms."

"But where did you hide the baby Jesus?" I asked her the day before her wedding. She was marrying George, a former priest, who dressed as badly as she did, and they were going to Honduras, where no one would care how they were dressed as long as they kept handing out condensed milk and vitamin bread. "Hah," Jacqueline said, in answer to my question, "that's between me and the Lord. I don't think I'll ever tell any-one." "Not even George," I asked, "not even your husband?" "George doesn't need to know," she answered. "It's enough that the baby Jesus brought us together."

I put my head in my hands and moaned. "Oh," I said, "Oh brother."

But I will say this, she looked pretty good for a forty-year-old, plump former nun, in her wedding dress made of the cheapest, shiniest, tackiest material you could ever imagine.

Before she and George got on the bus for the airport, she dug an elbow into my ribs and said, "Mysterious ways, don't forget. Mysterious ways."

GLORY B. AND THE ICE-MAN

Call this one yourself, I won't say one way or the other. What I'll do is, I'll present the facts. The facts and some commentary where it counts, but I won't say anything except what needs to be said to give a clear picture.

Bear in mind, Katasha has always had a feel for men even sadder and messier than herself.

Her apartment is like a warehouse for electronic hardware. The men who patronize Lil's on Canal Street are mostly discount salesmen. Canal Street is discount heaven and Lil's specialty is discount tits and ass. There, Katasha looks good. All the gadget salesmen are really fond of her. They want to comb her hair. They want to send her to data entry school. Katasha says, "They want me to die in their arms."

What they give her is factory rejects, free. Toasters, microwaves, vcrs, tape decks, cd players, woofers, tweeters, shaving cream warmers; Katasha keeps them all stacked up. Some addict is going to break in there and think he's died and gone to heaven, especially because of her latest.

"Come see my latest," she called down to me, so I puffed up

the clanking narrow stairwell. Her latest was the biggest color television I had ever seen, all screen and almost no console. "Forty inches," Katasha said, "new and improved."

She made popcorn, which came out black, and we sat down to look at the screen, which was so clear and flat it seemed like a window onto an alternate world. But Katasha didn't like what she saw.

We were watching a Science/Nature/Animal show on PBS. Back in the 1840s this man named Lord Franklin got an expedition together to find the Northwest Passage. I was in the bathroom getting black popcorn out of my teeth so I missed how they got lost, but get lost they did. The show documented how a recent scientific expedition was using these old maps to pinpoint the exact location of the graves of three crew members. The plan was to dig them up and autopsy them to see whether or not they had died of lead poisoning from eating out of soldered cans. Katasha sat straight up, looking at the bland, reasonable face on the forty-inch screen explain how the portable radiology device would be able to measure the lead content in the bones of the men they were going to unearth. "What?" she said, "what are they going to do?"

I explained to her that the scientists were going to dig up the bodies that had been buried in the ice for 130 years to see why they had died. "They can't," Katasha said through clenched teeth, "who gave them permission? Who gave them permission to do this thing?"

Coffins appeared. The men wiped ice and snow off to reveal the inscriptions. The first one said that the deceased was only seventeen years old. They opened up the coffin and unwrapped the many layers of stiff frozen cloth that were

wrapped around the corpse. There was a lot of cooing and exclaiming over the good condition of the subjects.

When the camera showed the body of the first subject, it was indeed remarkably well-preserved. More well-preserved, in fact, than certain people I've seen walking around on the streets. The lips were pulled way back from the corpse's teeth in a somewhat unsettling but expected rictus grin, the nose was blue and swollen, and the eyes seemed to look up out of deep, bruised, black sockets. But for a 130-year-old corpse it was looking pretty good. The scientists thought so, too. They were almost jumping out of their thermal suits with admiration and wonder. It was almost as if to none of these earnest, dedicated men had occurred the simple notion that, in fact, proven once again, things do keep better when stored in a cold place.

That was the thing about the corpse. It looked cold. It would be blue and cold and frozen forever, is the impression that corpse gave. Katasha threw black popcorn at the screen, "Put him back," she ordered, hissing through her gritted teeth, "put him back."

They did put him back, the corpse of that seventeen-year-old sailor, as they put back the other corpses, with a respectful little ceremony, all the scientists standing there with their ski caps off, but not until they had stretched out the dessicated body, x-rayed it, and photographed it from every conceivable angle. The cause of death was likely tuberculosis, but there was in fact a high lead content revealed in the bones.

The scientists speculated that Franklin and his sailors were all brain-damaged and insane from lead poisoning or the disastrous decision would not have been made to keep going farther and farther into that unknown white subzero territory,

with the crew perishing and ship-crushing icebergs lying in wait. Driven mad by lead, Franklin must have been blind to common sense, the prayers of the crew, and the safety of their lives, and though he should have turned back, he screamed in his hoarse cracked voice, "ONWARD!"

Lead poisoning was one explanation for such behavior, but then again maybe it was just being English. "Maybe that explains the British Empire," I tried to tell Katasha. "Lead poisoning," but she wasn't having any.

She snapped off the television. "You don't get it," Katasha said, "you missed the point completely." When I asked her what the point was, she sighed and whistled, as if amazed at the hugeness of my stupidity. "To die, so far from your home," she said, "in that place. That's not enough, they have to dig you up. They don't even make you any warmer. They just dig you up and put you back. I'm going to do something. I'm going to do something about this."

I told Katasha there was nothing that needed to be done, nothing she could do anyway. She answered by pulling a cassette out of the VCR and waving it in my face. "Oh, oh yes? Well, Miss Do-Nothing-But-Yawn-And-Scratch, Miss Why-Bother-Everything-Is-Already-Fucked, there is plenty I can do. Because I've got it all on tape. Besides," she added, "the guy said if I remembered to take my medication there was no reason I couldn't do anything I wanted." As usual she kicked me out of her apartment; all my visits ended that way.

That night it was too hot to sleep, and above me I could hear Katasha playing with her tape; the garbled shrieking of the

rewind, the hum of the fast forward. She was at it for hours, it seemed, forward, back, forward, back, as if she were looking for something.

I didn't see Katasha for three days after that, and it was a good thing because it was over a hundred degrees each day and I was in no mood for nonsense.

When she walked into my kitchen, I was sitting in front of the open refrigerator, in my underwear. "My boyfriend is visiting me," she announced.

"Oh yes, Katasha," I said, looking into the fridge, "that's nice, which boyfriend is that?"

A voice from the hallway with a thick, not-American accent said, "Can I come in now?"

"My boyfriend," Katasha mouthed at me silently, and then yelled out that the door was unlocked.

The door pushed open and Katasha's boyfriend stood in the entrance to my apartment. His eyes were fastened on her like a desperate dog. He had rather large, pale blue eyes.

"This is Alfred," Katasha said. I was not interested. "Alfred is a junkie," I told her. "What's that in your glass?" she asked me, nodding at my scotch with melting ice, the one I kept pressing against my forehead, "maple syrup?"

From the doorway Alfred asked, "What is a junkie?"

Now I really wasn't interested. I was not interested in his thick, possibly Scottish accent. I was not interested in his woolen hat pulled down over his ears, or the sweater he had pulled down over his hands, here in my kitchen, here in August. I was so uninterested it made me sleepy. "Alfred," I said, "do you want to come in and stop blocking the doorway?"

He looked harder at Katasha, who said, "He's waiting for you to close the refrigerator."

I pushed the refrigerator door shut with my foot, and in walked Alfred. He really didn't care about looking macho, because he sat on the floor at Katasha's feet and put his head in her lap. She took off his cap and patted his head. He hadn't washed his hair for a while, that was for certain.

"Well," I said, "well, Alfred. How long have you been in the States?" Katasha answered for him. "He's just visiting," she told me, still patting his head.

"Oh," I ooohed, "you guys must have known each other from before, then. Pen pals. Funny postcards with pictures of overweight cuddly things on them?"

Alfred spoke, and his voice had a strange sound, like an echo of something very close by, as if his voice weren't really speaking *now*, but a few seconds before, so that no matter what, it was a voice that could not be answered. "Katy is a good woman," his voice said, "she keeps me warm."

That was it for me, I was no longer passively uninterested, I was actively bored. "Listen, kids," I said, "I feel like being alone just this moment if you don't mind too much." They stood up and shuffled over to the door, holding hands. What impulse took hold of me I don't recall. Most likely I was driven to distraction by the boredom that had settled over me like an extra layer of damp heat. This made me say, "Nice to meet you, Alfred," and reach out to shake his hand.

You've guessed it already of course. I don't know why I'm bothering; you already know about Alfred's hand. Alfred's hand was cold. You know that, but you can't know how cold.

It was like touching a silver ice tray with the palm of your hand. It was like holding a piece of frozen tuna, but colder. It's also hard to describe the cognitive jolt that went from his hand to mine, because, while I held it, I knew—against all logic— that I was touching something that was very, very far away.

Katasha stood at the door. "Bye bye," she said, and gave me a little wave.

I didn't visit her again for a week. By then the heat spell had broken, and it was back to being only reasonably unpleasant.

"Where's your boyfriend?" I asked her. "Oh," she said, "him. He had to leave. It's OK though, I was starting to get a little tired of sharing my apartment. It's so small."

"Really," I said, "small."

"He left me a present though," she said. "It's in the freezer."

I opened the freezer door, as you can imagine, very, very slowly.

At first it seemed there was nothing at all in there, but then I saw it, stuck to the bottom. It was a piece of ice, clear as a diamond without facets, shaped like a heart. I loosened it from the freezer and picked it up. There were words carved into it, in small script. "For Katy," it said. It showed no sign of melting in my hand.

So listen. I'm not saying yes and I'm not saying no. I'm just saying that that girl could always attract the wrong guy. That girl could attract the wrong guy from a long, long way off.

He said he was an architect, and I believed him. He looked about forty years old, nicely done, Boston blue-blood accent, wrinkled seersucker jacket, premature white hair, like an early snow. He bought me vodka, insisted on ordering a name brand, said for fifty cents more why not drink the good stuff. I had almost no money that night, having paid the rent and gone to sleep for two days, so I told him that, whoever he was, I was glad to see him. It wasn't until I took a good look at his eyes that I saw how drunk he was. He was in the middle of a long binge, is what it looked like, the kind I've always secretly wished to go on myself, the kind of drunk that goes beyond inebriation into a state of almost genteel lucidity.

I knew that whatever we talked about, whatever happened, he wouldn't remember any of it.

When he talked he leaned his face into mine, far too close, and I took a good look at his eyes, which were lashless and pale blue.

My guess, he said, is that you have a very tall Yugoslavian boyfriend who deals black-market blue jeans behind the Iron

Curtain and would kill any man who looked at you twice, without a second thought.

Close, I said. Danger is my acronym. Death is my boyfriend.

Oh that's good, he giggled, putting up his hands movie marquee style, "Death. Is. My. Boyfriend." What's your name?

Gloria Bronski.

Gloria Bronski, do you know anything about cancer of the nerves?

Ah, I said, the old nine-to-five, the desire for *excelsior* . . .

Do you find me rude? He opened his eyes wide, aggression and ennui doing battle for his posture. Do you think you're a tough little bit?

I didn't answer him; I hummed along with the jukebox.

Listen, he clenched my hand, do you know Bess, the landlord's daughter, she's dead. Though she didn't die for me . . . He swayed, a cross between a wounded matinee gunfighter, *you got me*, and a cobra convincing some small mammal that its destiny was to be his dinner.

What, he said, seeing some odd thing in my face, surely you're not afraid of me, toothless old bastard like myself?

No, I'm afraid you'll stop talking to me and buying me drinks and I'll have to go home. I'm afraid to go home.

Self-revealing truths, when said at a certain time in a certain way, become lies, harmless small talk, insomniac chatter.

Don't worry, he said, I never leave a damsel in the same state of distress I found her in. You know me, I'm a gentle troubadour. He began to sing in Spanish, the only word I could make out was "corazón."

Listen, Corazón, the bartender said, friendly as ever, you need to go home, or get some air, don't you think?

No, quoth the gentle troubadour, give me another one.

The bartender shrugged, exactly like I used to when presented with such a customer, and poured him another drink. But what did he pour? Club soda. With a twist of lemon, nothing else. If this guy wasn't drunk, if he hadn't been drinking, he was clearly mad in some frightening and confusing way that I couldn't begin to approach. Instead, I pictured his brain shiny iridescent black, like the back of a Japanese beetle. He put his hand around my arm, like a bracelet, just below the elbow.

Come with me, I want to show you something.

What is it? I asked, reluctant to leave the bar before last call.

It's Coney Island, he replied, not missing a second.

We walked outside and he went into the fruit store on the corner of Second Street. Apples, green pears, lemons, and purple grapes tumbled out of the bins like jewels, hosed down and shining, tended by the owner's son who worked with his kick-ass cash-register mother and father all night, and was up and on his way to law school in Queens every morning at six. When I saw those no-bullshit Korean faces and caught a glimpse of all that fruit spilling over abundantly almost out into the street, I was ashamed for myself, of my indolence, my bone-crushing indolence, until he came out with a bag of strawberries.

He moved under the fake white moon of the streetlight and popped one into my mouth.

You can have all you want, he said.

I sat in his car, watched the lights from the Kiev Diner

on Seventh and Second. Yellow-gold and open all night. Soon to vanish.

The traffic signals changed from red to green to yellow to red and I thought about how nobody could afford to live here anymore, not anymore. I think I might have even curled up a little for a catnap in the back seat, drowsing off between eating strawberries.

He came down from his sublet about ten minutes later and tossed a piece of cloth at me. It was a bathing suit, olden style from the fifties, a one-piece thing with a fluted skirt and a purple plaid pattern.

Wear it and be wonderful, he told me.

Oh no, I bitched, you don't really want me to wear this thing.

Yes, he grimaced and started the car, and there I went again, floating over the Williamsburg Bridge while he tried to connect with the Brooklyn Queens Expressway, heading out toward Coney Island and the Atlantic Ocean. . . . It seemed so silly, pathetic even, but I knew what was waiting for me back at apartment 6-c, Pitt Street, and it was no joke. I decided not to go back there until the light was full blaring afternoon and there was no chance of being able to think about what I was going to look like sitting alone in that apartment when I was seventy years old and didn't even like cats.

My friend was talking about Beethoven as he drove, pushing his free hand through his snowfall hair. I'd like to be able to look him in the eye right now, he was saying, and tell him "Ludwig, you don't have to be afraid. I am your friend." Women don't like Beethoven, do they?

I don't know much about classical music.

Because he was ugly, ugly shows in the music. Let's face it, a woman wants a man with a little glamour to him, she wants a handsome man above all else.

I flashed a mental picture of him sitting drinking club soda in some cafe in Barcelona, watching the slowly diminishing back of a familiar female form as it disappeared down the sunny dusty street on the arm of a slender young bullfighter.

The image was hackneyed and horrible, it needed something stronger than club soda to make it work. I began to shake.

Look in the back seat.

What?

Look in the back seat, he didn't exactly shout, but merely raised his voice.

I did what he told me and there in the back under the beach towels was a fifth of the good stuff, which he didn't drink, so what was it doing there? It must've been a present for me.

After the first swallow I began to notice the houses peering over the parkway as we drove by. Seagulls described thin black arcs around the silhouetted chimneys and roof antennas.

When we got there it was five-thirty in the morning and except for a stray jogger, looking mechanical and disoriented on the boardwalk, we were the only ones there. The parachute and the roller coaster stood behind us like giant wind-polished skeletons, and the apartment buildings as always faced the sea: weary sentries, ossified guards to a kingdom of air.

I threw a large towel around myself and wiggled out of my clothes into the purple plaid bathing suit.

Are you going in? I asked him.

No, I'll just watch.

He sat there on the towel, on the beach, in the middle of a hot August early morning with his wrinkled jacket and his tie not even loose.

There was something in his eyes that was too abrasive to look at, his gaze when it fell on me was like a scrape.

I took some more vodka as an antiseptic, afraid that whatever he had was catching, and walked down to the water.

After the first moment of chill it was hardly cold at all. I dove under and held my breath for as long as I could, coming up gasping and treading water as I looked at the city on the shore. A city with everything. Coney Island its own set of fragile ruins.

I walked slowly back to where he was sitting, aware that he was watching me walk, watching me walk toward him in that bathing suit. He didn't turn his head when I sat down next to him but continued looking toward the water. I could have easily told him what a middle-aged run-of-the-mill loony toon he was and how he'd go back to his job in the architectural firm on Broome Street and they'd all laugh at him about the circles under his eyes and wonder if he'd fallen off the wagon.

Instead I said nothing at all because I didn't quite know how to phrase the words into the kind of acceptable and even flirtatious contempt I could usually use to my best advantage. I squeezed the water out of my hair and so didn't hear what he said next.

What?

He changed neither the direction he was looking in nor his expression, but I had the feeling he was speaking while doing something else, like trying to breathe through a rock instead of through air.

She's not coming back, is she? he said.

I thought about it.

No, I answered him, I don't expect she is.

We looked out in the same direction, out just beyond where our eyes could see, right behind the blue line of sky meeting water was the place where they'd all gone. All the people who weren't coming back. They were full of the grace of their various abandonments, they were far more beautiful than we were. I asked him to please drive me home.

2

My darling, it's haunted here:

In downtown Minneapolis the souls of the good dead become electric: streetlights or the tiny white jewels threaded in loops to the black sky lining the iron bridge across the Mississippi river. But look out: lead the wrong kind of life and you'll turn into one of the newly installed port-a-johns in Boom Island Park. And the lights are not confined to downtown: Minneapolis proper is twenty miles long and fifteen miles wide, so at night when the windows and lights are blinking, it seems to go on forever. The prospect of endless suburbs and bedroom communities sprawling out into the droning nighttime distance becomes both more and less overwhelming when you know that each light you see used to have a name.

The noise in downtown Minneapolis spins like pinwheel sparklers in your ears on Saturday night—televisions blaring out of sports bars, street hassles, rich-kid revelers lurching from club to club, radio-station songs of dance & romance, bright and twinkling like aluminum foil, the endless thudding of trucks over the Hennepin Avenue Bridge. But listen closely for

only a second and you will hear the calm electric buzz of the happy dead who just couldn't bear to leave the city, death unlike life sending down nothing that a soul can't bear.

In the suburbs it's quieter, but just as active. Three miles out of town, the malls menace and the industrial parks rule in air-conditioned silence over acres of implacable green lawns landscaped like golf courses. These areas used to be farms and rolling prairie and dotted woods, and when a man or a woman died there she shone in the stars overhead, relieved at last from the iron drudgery of farm work, but unable to let go of what had extracted, over the years, all her willing or unwilling love. So in the constellations over the Ridgedale mall the stars hang in frozen white-blue tears.

The rush of invisible homebound traffic on the other side of the sound wall carries the future in its drone and whisper: Listen, the traffic will tell you, this is a town that isn't going to be a town much longer, soon it will be a theme park whose intention is to recreate the days when there *were* towns, and men had jobs in them so they could buy small houses where their families would be relatively safe, except from whatever went on inside them, including the secret familial events not useful in illuminating the theme park's basic premise which will be this: America Is Full Of Towns Just Like This, Foaming Happily With Hardworking Citizens Who Know Their Way Home. This is the oracle droned by the sleeping sound of the cars on the main artery out of downtown and into the suburbs, a monotonous and irresistible song.

So it's fair to wonder if Minneapolis is still a city at all, if it even exists except as a concept. What do they have in

Minneapolis, what single thing do they have that would make people stay here, where the town is crusted with defunct machinery and empty grain elevators? Even the drugs here are lousy, costing five times as much as they would in any seaboard city. Not that people don't do them, because as you know, they surely do. Drugs are as inevitable as mega-malls in their own way, creating the same kind of helpless allegiance. The drug of alcohol, especially, available as it is, totally legal with no questions asked and without the huge import taxes that saddle other chemicals.

But here is where it gets brilliant beyond belief: for the cure of addiction to any chemical you can name, Minneapolis is the place to go. From all over the country come drug addicts with the means, or whose families have the means, to travel far from the scene of the accident and start over again. It seems like there are twenty-seven different treatment centers in down-town Minneapolis alone: wend your way through them and you can see anything from crackheads to connoisseurs of the finest East Asian opiate products. The crackheads are usually black and court-ordered, here to avoid jail sentences five times longer than the white clients in treatment for powder cocaine. The mostly-white clientele of the metro area's treatment centers are difficult to identify except as white-people-with-means, and although to the black people observing them they may appear as a group, to themselves they appear as a stunningly eclectic array of individuals with nothing in common except what's currently called "the disease of addiction."

The point of all this is that Minneapolis might not disappear as long as people keep coming to settle down here after com-

ing to recover. Creates a kick in the pants of the tax base, no doubt. And harms no one, only causes irritation on the part of the natives, who do not understand why the influx of so many people from the east and west coasts needs to be accompanied by the affects they had developed there. There was a time, say the older citizens of Minneapolis, when you could sit in a restaurant without the person at the next table waving their hands around to illustrate a point and talking so loudly you were sucked into a maelstrom of involuntary eavesdropping.

The lights of the city continue to watch the changes with absolute freedom from concern. They love this wretched town. They look at the citizens, old and imported, with worried amusement, the only emotion that ghosts are allowed. Undoubtedly the souls of the dead in Minneapolis are in our corner, but what can they do about any of it? They watch, they listen, and sometimes someone getting out of a car will look up at the white pinpoints garlanding a warehouse, or a car dealership, and they will feel a strange sense of comfort. Mostly not, though.

Certainly I'm no citizen. Of here, or of anyplace else. Still, I'm gambling that my whole life has led me here, for whatever reason, and that the city will at least tell me some stories. If I can make any sense of them at all, I'll tell them to you.

In the freightyard over in Northeast, the Burlington Northern boxcars gather and hook up, groaning in that woeful metal singing voice of iron scraping iron. In a scattered flock by the gathering trains, seventeen-year-old boys light up their bombers, drink blackberry brandy, and talk about what they'll do when they leave Minneapolis for the Big Town, which is Los Angeles, maybe, or even Chicago. Not by any of these trains, though, which are rusted iron boxes full of grain or Dixie cups or cans of artichoke hearts. They'll be leaving from the airport, thanks, wearing NBA jackets, stewardesses serving them beer and sex and sex and sex. In the meantime, with their red-veined eyes they stare at the yellow caution light and the pot seems to make it glow golden like a glob of molten metal, or like the sun boiling in the black reaches of space. They reassure themselves that it's only a light saying caution, but what it's really saying is a little more complicated, even if the gist of it is similar to its mechanical intention:

Caution, it says. Peligroso. Danger. Do Not Jump On Tracks. Do Not Go See A Blockbuster Action Film in which

the Nautilized hero falls down flat under a slowly moving train, the audience pretending to think he's dead but really just waiting to see how he gets out of it and big surprise, man, the train passes harmlessly an inch and a half over his head. Do not get into an apricot-schnapps-fueled argument with Harly Knudson and Steven Kochevsky over whether or not you could, man, you could actually do that. And when they dare you and Kochevsky calls you a faggot in front of the girls who show up who are probably too wastoid to notice anyway, don't try to give a live 3-D site demonstration of how lacking in fear and weighted down with your own huge testicles you are.

The papers will blip it in the metro section, Knudson and Kochevsky not interviewed because they say they weren't there. Morning DJs will read the article on the morning show and make jokes about evolution weeding out the stupid ones, and your mother will never smile without clenching her teeth again.

The general consensus in this neighborhood on the whole incident, from what I can gather, which isn't much, since no one is particularly keen on talking to an outsider who just moved in three years ago, is that Jeffrey DiScelli was always a strange boy, and that Harly and Steven shouldn't be penalized for his peculiarities, especially since they were, respectively, right and left wing for Edison varsity hockey. Looking good this year, too. At least so far.

Sometimes, and this grieves me to say, I dislike my neighbors just as much as they would dislike me if they ever found out who I really was. Sometimes however, I can tolerate them,

like the time I had a broken ankle and the woman across the street came over with a big pot of stew that lasted from Sunday until the following Thursday. I don't think she would have come over if she'd known my health status. Not that her son might not turn out the same as me, since he's spent the past fifteen years since high school hanging at that bar where intravenous methamphetamine is the order of the day, coming home to Mom's house at one o'clock in the afternoon, with a gaze like a cornered stallion: mean and terrified. He and his buddies sometimes spend all night working on the cars set up in the backyard, drinking beer, all talking at once in the sharp, low tones of serious business. His mother ignores it and keeps making stew in her cluttered yet clean little kitchen.

I am so far from home, here in Minneapolis, that I might in fact be an entirely different person. No. That's just wishful loneliness speaking. You can take the girl out of wherever, but you can't take wherever out of the girl. Except, I hear, in California, where people get instant new identities, free of cultural or familial baggage, the second they cross the state line. Now be realistic, and don't romanticize. There is no way the HIV-positive Jewish child of professional intellectuals is going to be beloved to a group of conservative working-class Polish Catholics.

Why am I here then? Oh, the housing—the housing so beautiful and inexpensive that I can afford my very own little cottage here in this undiscovered gem of a neighborhood. I'm a one-girl invasion. Today, me; tomorrow twenty-five charming little cappuccino-serving bistros. So far the trend hasn't quite caught fire, but it's only a matter of time. Then I will casually mention at every opportunity that I used to live here

long before it was cool. Everyone, the real working citizens and the trendy new transplants, will be sick to death of me.

And so many, many things can't find me here. So many things that would never think to look for me here, and wouldn't want to come here if they did. I have disappeared from sight. Slipped under the radar of my mother and father and their heartbroken concern and questions about how I'm doing. The doctors and lawyers and doctoral candidates and Harvard-to-Hollywood publishing moguls whose ranks I was supposed to have joined fifteen, sixteen years ago are not relevant here, and in fact they might as well not exist. Yes. I'll say it to all the people who have ever done better than me in the snagging of golden statues and security: you might as well not even exist. Now leave me alone with my bitterness and resentment or I'll say something to make you feel uncomfortable, and don't think I won't do it.

Life goes on. I go out, I go to community board meetings, I go to the stadium-sized supermarket, I come back home. I deposit my monthly disability check. I come back home. It's good not to have a job right now, but soon I'll be back in the workforce, with everyone else who is forced to work.

Like a strange breeze, however, Jeffrey DiScelli sometimes keeps me company. Looking out my kitchen window I can see the lights of the Northeast freightyards, and I can hear the boxcars backing up and reconnecting. Yellow and white lights are threaded sparsely through the tops of wire fences. Jeffrey DiScelli is there, a young boy now for a long time, with no need to be popular, just watching with slightly startled eyes, easily mistaken for the lights meant to caution traffic.

On an early Sunday morning a reporter called to ask me questions about women with AIDS. Don't waste your time with me, I told her, I'm nothing more in the scheme of things than a rather charming statistical anomaly.

Meaning?

Meaning I come from a wealthy family, supportive, who provided me with a safety net, its resemblance to a spiderweb notwithstanding. I don't have children, I don't have problems getting access to medical care, I don't have to buy the groceries for the family when I'm too exhausted to stand up for more than ten minutes straight, and I don't have a husband who will feel betrayed enough to resort to physical expression if the house is still cluttered and dusty at the end of the day. I don't have your usual problems, in other words, either girl- or boy-style. Go talk to somebody else.

For instance, I suggested, you could talk to Amelio. He repaired broken air conditioners and refrigerators, a trade he picked up upstate—upstate being how a certain East Coast demographic refers to prison, the prisons being mostly upstate.

I hooked up with him mainly because he was half Puerto Rican and he looked entirely Puerto Rican and therefore must've had access to drugs. He was the kind of Puerto Rican man I could relate to, not like most Puerto Rican men, who seemed mainly involved in going to work, taking out the garbage, and teasing their children.

He was also just the kind of boy I *would* hook up with. His heart was in the right place for being a street-smart tough guy, but his physique was unsuited. He was bird-skinny, with painful shoulder blades and long-lashed emerald eyes. Beautiful, but girly-girl. When we walked together on the street, if anyone said anything to me he would draw himself up and issue a series of threats. During the time that I knew him his nose got broken once and his ribs fractured several times.

We drove around in his employer's van at night when I could sneak out of one of the places I was staying—either my boyfriend's or my parents'. I didn't allow him to meet my parents, naturally. They'd put up with men who had beaten me up, they'd put up with thirty-three-year-old homeless musicians, they'd put up with painters who constantly asked them to invest in their art, but they would not put up with air conditioner repairmen, they would not put up with someone who looked like he was coming to do apartment maintenance. My parents are intellectuals.

Amelio often said he loved me, and I liked him very much. He had a sweet spirit, and as much of a fuck-up as he was, he had a certain bravery. Even when we were in the early stages of opiate withdrawal he managed to stay cheerful, but I began to see less of him when it became apparent that outside of his van,

which was a good place to fix, he was as much of a liability as an asset. He never had any money. I told him I was going to have sex with a local drygoods merchant, in the neighborhood where we went to buy drugs, on an exchange basis. I was still well enough then that I could consider the arrangement. "If you do that I will tell everyone that you are a slut," he said regretfully. Who was "everyone," I wondered; who did he know that knew me outside of one or two passing junkies with whom our exchanges were limited to "you know what's open?" and "they'll be back in five minutes they said."

Amelio, feeling flush, once brought me some flowers which we put in a can of water on the dashboard of his van, and after that I didn't see him for a while.

The next time I heard from him was when the wife of a friend of his called me saying he'd given the friend my number as a possible source of bail. My boyfriend, who was ready to kick me out of his apartment, hovered ragefully over my shoulder as I took the call. He knew what was up. My parents knew what was up. Money was missing everywhere, and they wouldn't let me in the house. I didn't want to stay on the street, having no skill for it. I was considering suicide, but I wanted to die happy, and that would take drug money, which, in turn, would take time and effort to come by. In other words, it was a normal day. "Sorry, can't help you today."

He called a week later while my boyfriend was out. I was in a better mood, having obtained what I needed to want to live a little longer and having injected it into a vein in my wrist about ten minutes earlier. "Why are you in jail?" "Well, you

know. I was driving the wrong car at the wrong time. Listen," he went on, "sometimes some of the girls send us stuff in here. A pair of your panties, a ribbon from your hair, whatever." I told him I'd see what I could do. I rarely wore underwear and my hair was too short for ribbons. Women only wore ribbons in their hair in old songs, anyway. The poor man, to have only me for his idea of a woman out there. "Don't call me again, though," I said. "I'll write to you. My boyfriend gets angry." "I thought you said he didn't mind?" which was something I'd told him once when I was expecting him to call with some dope, to bypass all the bullshit.

Things were getting a little more desperate in my corner. My boyfriend was certainly going to kick me out any minute if I couldn't think of any more excuses about missing objects and pawn tickets. The phone rang during one of our morning conversations.

"It's Amelio. Listen, sweetheart, I have to tell you something."

"Amelio," I said, with one eye on my boyfriend who was pointing to the door he wanted me to walk out of with $1.15 in my pocket and a January sleet-storm spattering the street, "I told you not to call me."

"Okay," he said, with perfect equanimity, and hung up.

Do you have to be a brilliant plot-predictor to guess what it was Amelio had to tell me, and how he thought I should know and go get the test? No you do not, and in hindsight there's not a doubt in my mind what news Amelio had to share. What he was trying to do was the decent thing. Now,

eight years later, where is Amelio? You might as well ask me a question on quantum physics. He had no girlfriend, no mother, no father, no friends who could come and see him. He may have died there, he may have died soon after, he may still be alive, spending his life shuttling between methadone and medical clinics. I'm living in the love of my family and the bosom of my world. I live within the warm, firelit circle of privilege, under a whispering midwestern sky that blushes down on the snow-crushed streets these January mornings.

So don't ask me anything about it. Find Amelio for me. Ask him. Tell him I say hello from Minneapolis.

3

Kostelowicz and I listen to the radio on Sunday nights until two o'clock. My eyes become glazed and prickly like dusty grapes, but Kostelowicz has long ago abandoned regular patterns of sleep and wakefulness; he's eighty-one years old, he's outlived the entire concept of circadian rhythm. We tried to watch TV once—Kostelowicz has cable—but it didn't work out. Two minutes of MTV and the fifty-one years between us reared up like a thousand-year war. It was Madonna who did it. There she was, backlit like a gem on velvet, wearing a gold leotard with breast cups engineered by some demented Frank Lloyd Wright disciple. The music was thumping and she was running her hand up and down between her well-articulated thighs. Kostelowicz gave a disbelieving bark: "She's playing with herself!" "You can look at it that way," I said, "or you could look at it like a cultural critic and say she's redefining the metaphor of female sexuality as it's traditionally been presented to us." "I wouldn't say anything ungentlemanly, Gloria," Kostelowicz answered, gripping his walker with knucklebone hands, the backs of which are speckled and fierce, like mackerel,

"but you're a thirty-year-old woman. You've been married and divorced, you've lived in the world, you know perfectly well (a little clank on the floor here with the walker) that woman is playing with herself." "Well, she's one of the richest women in America," I mentioned. "She's worth hundreds of millions of dollars. She has an incredible amount of power."

"Turn off that box," Kostelowicz sighed, "I'm going to have a heart attack." I turned off the tube and switched on the radio: KTLO and the *Señor Cómico* show. Not that I stopped talking. Kostelowicz is an old man, without many visitors. He doesn't mind if I talk, he doesn't mind being badgered by my worldview, which changes from minute to minute, depending on what comes over the airwaves. In this way he's what I've always longed for: a captive audience.

When I was a child I couldn't sleep at night. Nothing terrified me more than being awake, in my room upstairs, after my parents and everyone else in the city and on the planet was asleep. Even with the light on I seemed to inhabit a world of inanimate objects: furniture and the cold white streetlights outside combined a lack of emotional existence with malevolent intent. I didn't know that was a paradox; I was eleven years old. The lamps, the bookshelves, the windows seemed to take on sharp edges and to wish me evil. Thinking about the furniture would lead me to thinking about death; when I was dead I wouldn't exist any more than a marble vase would, and it would be forever. I was afraid of death, and I felt that things wanted me dead. Every creak, every sound of settling floorboards would make me shriek. I often cried and called for my

mother, shamefully pleading for her to wake up and come into my room. She would bring warm yellow light flooding into the doorway and make me forget instantly that there was going to be an end to anything. But she also needed her sleep and was starting to get upset with me. If, by an act of sheer will, I managed to let her sleep through the night, I would huddle under the sheets whispering dramatically, "morning, morning, won't you ever come?"

That year, in one of their many attempts to make me happy and keep me safe at night, my parents bought me an AM/FM radio.

The idea was for me to be lulled to sleep by the music, but that was not quite how it went. I kept the volume low until eleven when I knew they had gone to bed and were no longer listening for signs of nocturnal activity from my room. Then I'd turn it up as far as I dared, which wasn't much, and lie on the floor with my ear to the speaker for the next three hours— at least until two, when the DJs changed shifts. Then, bleary-eyed and bleary-minded, I'd turn it down until I could hardly hear it, but never off. Turning off the radio was like turning off the lights or letting a campfire go out in the forest; it would let in the night and a world where no one, not even my mother, would love me.

For the first year I listened to the local pop station, taking comfort that the cheerful, idiotic sounds of reality and com-merce continued even when the world outside was empty as the moon. I liked the commercial jingles, the hearty baritones, the seamless, invisible transitions from weather to sports to Three Dog Night. I knew all the lyrics to the chorus of every top-ten on the charts, and the more they played a song, the better I liked

it. Hearing a song played three times in one hour was like seeing a friend 'round the corner in the lunchroom. No elaborate
greetings were necessary, but it was somehow reassuring. The
time would pass, and I would fall asleep safely, encircled by silly,
happy sounds. I was still hollow-eyed and drowsy all day at
school, but at least I was no longer terrified all night long.

When I was twelve or thirteen I started to explore new
territory on the dial. At first I'd turn quickly back to my home
station; what I heard on the others made me edgy. The songs
were longer, more instrumental, sometimes eerie. It took me a
few months of quick and timid listening experiments before I
could leave the dial on wcol, a station I'd heard called "pro-
gressive" by the college girl who helped my mother out on
Tuesdays. I got it: music for older kids, even grown-ups—
people like the college girl, who smoked marijuana, wore
Mexican jewelry, and had jobs working with the poor. The
kind of people I would someday be just like, if I didn't become
the only girl in the world to die of a heart attack before her first
period. Once I was able to categorize their target audience, the
whole idea of long instrumentals and mysterious segues
became familiar, nonthreatening. In this respect, at least, I was
an average American child, media-savvy and nervous. What
made me feel most savvy and excited was a breathy-voiced DJ
who did the ten-to-two shift on weeknights. She began each
shift with Andean flute music and a Kahlil Gibran poem,
which, at the time, I thought was wonderful. Due to the insin-
uating, ragged breathiness of her voice, she got a lot of corre-
spondence from her male listeners, often men who were incar-
cerated in one of the penal institutions within the station's

broadcast range. I liked it when she read their intense and lonely postcards on the air, but what I liked best was when, about halfway through her shift, she would exchange some banter with her engineer, Frank. "Here's Frank, bringing me a cup of the world's worst coffee.

"What's for lunch today Frank?"

"A tasty grinder from Lenny's. Eggplant for me, you get the vegetarian moussaka."

"How's Lenny tonight? I imagine he's devastated about the Mets' recent string of disasters."

I imagined myself at 2 AM, sitting in the sound booth with my fashionably cowboy-booted feet up on some convenient surface, tossing friendly jibes back and forth with Frank about baseball, delis, and vegetarianism, and the definition of cool.

I started making up my own radio station, W-L-U-V, W-LOVE, and in between French and math I'd sneak into the bathroom, look in the mirror, pack my voice down a couple of registers, and say, "This is Glory, coming to you on W-L-U-V, reminding you that life is just one stop on the longer journey. And speaking of journeys, we're going to be taking a little trip with the latest from The Moody Blues."

Of course, the popular girls overheard me doing this and proceeded to make my stop on the journey a hellish and humiliating one, but I was too sleepy to care much.

Often I didn't turn off the radio at two, but kept listening, just one more song after one more song all through the next DJ's shift.

My mother woke up early one morning and came upstairs to see me on the floor, knees hunched under flannel nightgown,

staring at the glowing green numbers on the radio dial.

"My God," she said, "have you been up all night? You have. I can tell by your eyes. You look like a fruit bat."

Then we leave the station's broadcasting range, and all we get is static, a steel-wool carpet of meaningless sound. It's an irritating noise and it lasts for seventeen years. When we finally pick up something intelligible, I'm in a boardinghouse in St. Paul, sitting in a room with an old man who's abandoned regular hours. What were they playing when the signal was down? Nothing that needs to be heard, and nothing to sing along with, certainly. Let's just say that the way I kept listening to just one more song was prophetic of my later inability to resist just one more of anything. This inability made it necessary for me to come to St. Paul. I'd never counted on living in this place, where the cold smashes you in the face every morning as if you'd walked into the side of a meat locker, but I hadn't counted, either, on wanting to live. It seemed like such a piddling ambition, like longing for a career in data processing. Especially for someone like me, obviously destined for greatness.

The truth is, I'd had it with greatness of any kind, and I was happy not to wake up in the morning with a knee-twitching spasm. I was happy not to wake up ashamed and desolate, in desperate need of money. I was happy to have a room at West Seventh, a boardinghouse divided into bedrooms with sinks and floored entirely in dark-green wall-to-wall that smelled like fungus. It was my room, I earned it, and because it was mine, I thought it was pretty.

I didn't meet Kostelowicz until I had been there for two weeks. He had the whole top floor to himself, with his own kitchen and separate entrance. He seemed to avoid the other tenants, who consisted mainly of outpatients from various state-run facilities. There were two men who, through the miracle of psychotropic medication, managed to appear simultaneously both doughy and thin, and one woman, obese and defensive. When I first moved in I tried to organize Monopoly games and offered to share my meals. It soon became clear, however, that this was only an intrusion, another demand. The house, always kept dark to save on electricity, was what they would come home to after working all day at fast-food restaurants. They would sit, exhausted, in front of the TV, eating their take-home dinners. In the dark living room they would watch the colored lights and let the volume batter them until, one by one, they drifted off. The TV was on eighteen hours a day, the only light in the house. Sometimes, from my room, I could hear the man downstairs barking in terrified laughter, or crying, "Don't . . . don't . . . I didn't." Well, what did I think it meant anyway, to be sick? One thing it meant was that you were alone. I was always one to blithely deny the facts of damage. At least everyone in the house had a job, including, most of the time, me. Sometimes that's the most you can ask, and sometimes that's asking quite a bit.

Not that I didn't have any friends, but I didn't like it at night, in the winter, in St. Paul, sitting in my room with a book, listening to the TV downstairs blaring the sound of exploding helicopters. Which is why when Kostelowicz caught sight of me coming up the back stairs and asked me in for

coffee and Bismarcks, it was all I could do to remember to hesitate. Old people scared me, especially old men. I suspected them of harboring sexual perversions. No, I'll be honest, I suspected them of harboring sexual drive, which revolted me the way a sexual perversion is supposed to revolt you. After I checked Kostelowicz for any unsettling bulges, any suspicious gaps in his pajamas revealing anything sad flopping out of a mournfully sparse patch of damp gray pubic hair, I decided that he seemed in no way perverted. But listen, the truth is I would have gone in anyway. Some nights the idea of an old man playing with himself just didn't seem like that much of a threat next to an evening without human chitchat.

His apartment was a surprise: It was not at all the dank, mildewed coven I had expected. In fact it was tastefully furnished. Of course by tastefully furnished I mean not furnished in the style of the working class. That's the kind of evil fascist I am. I doubt there's any hope for me. He had low-backed couches put out at angles and decent reproductions on the walls. On the end tables tall drinking glasses held fresh flowers.

"The Meals-on-Wheels girl is so kind to bring them," he told me when I let him get a word in edgewise. Of course I talk too much when I'm nervous, so you can imagine how I let the words fly at the old man, setting them loose like birds. I filled the room with piping, fluttering words, so that he wouldn't know that Gloria Bronski, babbling desperately for the past ten years of her life, had forgotten, if she ever knew, what to say to another human being. Kostelowicz laughed, sometimes, at my jokes, agreed with some of the things I said,

and politely disagreed with others. Outside of customer service exchanges at various temp jobs, it was the first time I'd talked to another human being in almost a week. When Kostelowicz asked if I minded the radio on, I said, "No. The radio? Are you kidding? The radio's my favorite thing in the whole world." I meant it when I said it, although I hadn't listened to the radio since I was eighteen, and nothing except chemically-induced euphoria had been my favorite thing for a long time.

I told Kostelowicz about my day during the commercial breaks on *Night Talk*. I tried to make it sound amusing, casting myself as the beleaguered heroine of a series of ludicrous mishaps on the way to a job interview. The interview itself was the real juice, though; I'd been saving the similes since three o'clock: "So after forty-five minutes this woman comes out, and I tell you she had the most enormous hair I've ever seen. You know the way they wear their hair now, like it's been laminated in the middle of being windtossed? Her smile is laminated, too. She's like a shiny smiling tombstone. Can you picture her? Like the Meals-on-Wheels lady if she was evil. She's got this high-pitched voice that sounds like talking shellac."

Kostelowicz's head had dropped forward, his forehead a pale speckled globe, his eyes shut, his breathing almost a snore. I took a deep breath and looked around, in an irrational reflex, making sure that there was no one else in the room. I would have whispered what I told him next, but whispering was not in my nature.

"The woman was fine, actually. She was nice. It was me. My shoes had mud on them, and I laughed too loud. I looked like a child. Anyone looking at me can tell I don't know how to do

even the simplest things. I don't know how to drive, what to say, how to get in a checkout line at a convenience store. And besides, I'm ugly. I just want to sit on my bed and look at photographs of when I was little." I was alarmed at the tears, which I felt not in my eyes, but in my throat, like a sharp breath.

Kostelowicz, who had not been asleep at all, but listening with closed eyes, cleared his own throat, and the tears vanished from mine.

"Ridiculous," he said. "You're a lovely and capable young woman."

"You don't know my whole story," I answered, starting to laugh. Kostelowicz snorted and said, "Well, I can imagine the worst. It still doesn't change my opinion."

We quieted down for a while, listening to *Night Talk*. The show actually goes all night, live; the host does a seven-hour shift. He discusses a topic with a guest, then takes callers. Their voices come in over the line, awkward, breathless, incensed, having planned exactly what they are going to say. Sometimes they are the voices of people with rattlesnake minds, venomous and panicked; they feel cornered by Jews, Indians, blacks, women who have had abortions, all the people they think are going to take things away from them. They say things like, "I mean, basically they bring it on themselves. Everyone has the choice to follow God's path, or not, and this is what happens." More often, though, people call in with their opinions, their fears, and within limits, their fantasies; and it's nothing that no one's heard before, nothing earth-shattering or frightening or astonishing. They say things like, "If people could remember to be considerate," or "My wife and I were married for thirty-

one years before she passed on and I'll tell you, the key is respect."

What's amazing to me is how well I understand the impulse: It's one in the morning and you have an opinion. You are awake and everyone else is asleep. You work the night shift, or you work someplace where no one wants your opinions, or you don't know how to express an opinion; you're afraid you'd look crazy, standing there babbling about your opinion. It's been so many hours since you've talked to anyone that your voice cracks when you open your mouth to speak. You've looked out your window hours before and the neighbors were calling to their children and standing in their yards drinking sodas; you've seen a man and a woman walk naked through their kitchen and make sandwiches. Other people's conversations flow around you in currents, and you are a rock in the stream, a rock with an opinion.

The DJ on *Night Talk* is good at his craft; he neither rushes nor indulges. I know his eyes are on the clock every second, but his voice is conversational. The people that call him are the people I would like to have a conversation with. I think, with the grandiosity inspired by a day of unpleasant job interviews, that I could cheer them up, make them laugh, make even the ones with violent minds see a little reason.

"That," I say to Kostelowicz, "is the job I want."

"So?" says the old man. He's put on his glasses and his eyes are huge behind the lenses; they look like two newborn things, his lashes gummed up and glistening.

"It's not that simple," I said. "First I'd have to apply for school. They'd send me a hundred pages of forms, and I'd have

to fill them all out correctly. That right there is a problem. Then I'd have three years till I got my BA, which would be just about worthless. I'd have to get a masters in communications, by which time I'd be thirty-five, and applying for gofer jobs at the local public service station, competing with people fifteen years younger than me for the same position."

"Well," Kostelowicz said, "in my opinion, it's worth any amount of trouble."

"What is?"

"Finding the right job. That would be the right job for you."

"How on earth do you know?" I asked.

"The way you light up my room," he says, "the way you light up my room with your voice."

PARACHUTE SILK

All right then, I'll make a list, one list with two separate headings: Things I Will Never Do, and Things I Would Never Do. The Things I Will Never Do preserve my sense of sorrow; the Things I Would Never Do preserve my sense of dignity. My sense of humor preserves itself, like a ghastly, encephalic curio sitting on a dusty shelf in the pitch-black basement of some madman's antique store. I wouldn't give it up, though, and you can put that under the Would Never heading—leaving space above it, naturally, for the more important things, like murder or boinking your best friend's sweetheart.

The Will Never list is much longer than the Would Never; almost anything can give me an idea for an item. The red silk parachute that Matthew left on the porch, for instance, reminds me that I Will Never jump out of an airplane, but that's a doubleheader—I Would Never jump out of an airplane, either. It's a conscious decision, one of the easier ones I've had to make. What kind of person would do that, and what do they get out of it, except a sense of relief when the thing opens correctly?

I'm already relieved, thank you, and—considering what I've done to myself—happy to be alive, if somewhat cranky in the mornings. I'm cranky in the mornings because at night, when I turn out my lights, when, according to my recovery counselor, you're supposed to concentrate on positive, relaxing images, what I get instead is a sort of cavalcade of hits: Gloria's Most Painful and Embarrassing Moments on Parade. It's especially bad if I remember all the times I made a fool of myself when I was drunk. Once that starts, I can be up for hours, snapping to my memories, "Go away." Just imagine some woman you saw in a bar once, hair tumbled and greasy, eye makeup hopeful the day before yesterday, loudly tossing inappropriate remarks into the closed circles of other people's conversations. Her charming and incisive bons mots land on the floor with an unpleasant splat, as if someone had just hurled a dead frog to the ground at your feet; you turn around, and there she is, smiling like the belle of the ball. If you wish she'd just go away, believe me, so do I. Here in Minnesota, Land of Ten Thousand Treatment Centers, they've got a program for any addiction you might care to name, but memories are something they can't do all that much about.

I didn't last that long as a rowdy drunkard, and when I switched to opiates at least I quieted down. In fact, I should quiet down right now and look over this list, which has gotten a little bit out of control. As a list, however, it's typical of me—Glory at her most self-centered, self-involved, self-pitying, and a list of other terms that start with my favorite word, "self."

My counselor had told me to write down a list of things that had to do with Matthew, who left the red parachute on my

porch—what I felt good about, what I felt bad about. I've been out of the halfway house for over a year, but I still take my counselor's advice. If this list isn't quite what she had in mind, it's because I've always had a creative approach to advice-taking.

But for the moment I'll reject creativity; I'll just do what they say—Get Honest, Talk About My Feelings. What I feel most strongly at this moment is a desire not to think or talk about Matthew. His name said aloud embarrasses me. It's like something that happened when I was six or seven, when I was playing with puppets in the office of one of the innumerable kiddies' shrinks my baffled and worried parents were sending me to. Because the puppets were birds, I was putting them into a nest. The shrink looked at me and said, "You know, Gloria, why you're doing that? Because you want a nest, too. You want someplace where you can feel safe and warm." I was overcome with revulsion—I felt as if he'd just stuck his hand up my dress—and I decided I hadn't heard his comment. I'm bringing up that little childhood idyll to illustrate how the name Matthew makes me feel at this very moment. But I'm too big a girl now to go on playing with puppets, pretending not to hear something.

To make myself really uncomfortable, I could make a list of the things I valued about Matthew. The first was his lack of glamour. When we began to spend time together in the occupational-therapy room of Sunrise House, I remember thinking that if I had not been an addict I would never have been there, hanging out with some dark, overweight guy who wore sandals and socks like a tourist from the Netherlands. Never even mind the sweaters his mother sent him.

In the program, we had to make lists of our own character defects. There were certainly some things I despised about myself. Two of these were a desire to be liked and a desire to be glamorous. Matthew told me that my desire to be glamorous was only the made-for-TV version of my desire to be liked, but he didn't quite get what I was saying; I had trouble explaining to him how much I loathed my own idea of what constituted glamour. That idea was by no means an unusual one: Like so many other kids gone wrong from my time, place, and class, I thought it glamorous to be self-destructive. Unfortunately, I had also always known that this was a stupid and callow way to think. I knew that self-destruction was a vile method of slumming; I knew that there were people who got destroyed whether or not they wanted to. Here was Glory, beloved baby girl of professional parents, going into neighborhoods her great-grandfather had worked all his life to get his family out of, sniffing around for heroin, the opiate of the people. Marie Antoinette in her little peasant dress, Glory in her leather jacket. I knew all this, and yet I couldn't stop. Matthew had other reasons for being unable to stop, but eventually we both couldn't stop simply because we could not stop, and we wound up in the OT room pouring out molds of ceramic owls—lucky for us. I say "lucky" because I'm not so far gone that I don't know there are many, many worse places to end up and worse things to have to do than Occupational Therapy.

Matthew looked, to me, like the kind of kid nobody would socialize with in school, like I'd been. As a penance for having wanted to hang out with the cool kids, I attached myself to him. We stayed up as late as we could, drinking decaf out

of Styrofoam cups and listening to Matthew's mix tapes on the tape recorder we snuck out of the office. The white fluorescent lamps overhead would hum, and eventually a night staffer would tell us to get to our rooms.

The staff told me to try to make friends with more women. I was a little insulted that they thought I hung out with Matthew because I couldn't get anybody better-looking to have an exclusive relationship with. Matthew would make me a tape every week, of songs from other tapes. From his selection of songs I would know, or think I knew, how he was feeling. How much did I really know, I wonder, about anything? I was thirty pounds overweight from the methadone I'd been on before and the antidepressants they had me on then. Between those and my AZT, I could hardly find my butt with both hands, as the old-timers like to say.

Eventually I became more lucid and ready for the outside world. Matthew did, too; armed with the Twelve Steps and our newly acquired Tools for Living, we graduated from the residence within days of each other. Matthew had asked me to come back to the House for his ceremony and be the one to give him his graduation medallion. But I was too busy: I'd dropped that thirty pounds by then and met a boy. At that point a boy wasn't much use to me, because of what I liked to call "my health status," but I was as excited as if every night were my first boy-girl movie date. If I kept things at that first-night level, I would not have to talk seriously with any boy about the risk of transmission; no one has to talk about condoms on a first date when she's sober.

Anyway, I sent Matthew a note instead. It was a charming

note, of course, but so what? Put that on a list of things I would like to have among my memories but don't: giving Matthew his graduation medallion.

Matthew was back at work two weeks after he got out. He had that going for him: He might not have been the guy to get into the VIP lounge at some glitter-trash night club, but he was fit for the aspects of life that I feared the most. While I bounced around among different service jobs, learning how to complete tasks and show up on time, Matthew was working at InfoSystem as a computer-repair troubleshooter. He'd worked for the head office in Detroit, and when he went into treatment his boss had gotten his insurance to pay for the cushiest among the many chemical-dependency centers that dot the Minnesota landscape. They'd held his position for him, then found him a transfer slot in the Cities. That was the kind of addict Matthew was: He'd used for five years before anybody was wise to him, and he was so good at his job that they overlooked the funds he'd fiddled. I admired him for his control, never having had any to speak of myself.

He said to me, "There's a lot of things about you that I admire, too, but they're probably not the things you would admire about yourself."

Some people don't like to be praised; apparently it makes them uncomfortable. I am not one of them. I like praise, and I like my praise specific, so I asked him, "What? What things?"

"I admire your ability to be someone I know well. That's not something I can do that easily—be someone anybody knows well."

Matthew's job was to drive around the Cities to various InfoSystem offices and help them fix their computers when they went down, which they did on a daily basis. Around lunchtime he was usually parked in his blue office-issue van near the capitol. I was doing phone-survey work in a place right there on Rice and Marion, so I'd step into his van and we'd eat sandwiches together in the front seat.

Usually our conversations were interrupted when Matthew's car phone buzzed and he had to talk some panicked office employee through the steps needed to get the system back up. "Do you have your system disk?" he would ask, his voice like sleep. Then, never altering the comforting lack of expression in his tone, he'd take them through all the logical procedures. "If anything else comes up, call me right back," he'd say, then he'd hang up the phone, looking away at the clumpy little skyline of downtown St. Paul.

"Do you have to do that on your lunch hour?" I asked him once, feeling foolish because I'd been in the middle of an animated bout of storytelling when the call came in.

"They're so scared when the system goes down," he said. "They're afraid they'll lose their jobs. I'm supposed to report all the calls, but I don't."

One evening in late March, Matthew showed up at my door with his latest mix tape and a bundle of things that he'd found in the closet of his new apartment. One of the things was the red silk parachute. "I thought you might want to use it for a bedspread, or a curtain," he said. "It reminds me of you."

In an uncharacteristic spasm of self-restraint, I didn't ask why. Instead, I suggested we take it outside on the porch.

It was windy that night, and not too cold—a miracle in Minnesota, where spring doesn't come until the very last minute. The next-door kids were still outside, clanking around on their one bike for the half-dozen of them. Looking down Dayton Avenue, Matthew and I could see the cathedral, with its oxidized-green dome looking like jade in the moon-white floodlights. The real moon floated above it, courteous and pale and distant, as a Minnesota moon would be. We held the chute over the side of the porch and the wind took it up with a definite, firm thunk. The red silk flew out, and we could feel it straining at our hands; it leaped and danced, like a flag. I had the feeling for a moment that we were sailing, Matthew and I, up over the cathedral. We weren't of course, and it wasn't really warm, so we went back inside. That's on the list for my counselor, that evening.

Another reason I valued Matthew was his honesty. Every single member of his family was in what is ominously referred to as "the program." They were in different branches of it, all over the country—branches that seemed to be growing and multiplying at a dazzling rate of speed: Overeaters Anonymous, Spenders Anonymous, Parents or Adult Children of Alcoholics Anonymous, Clutterers Anonymous, Love Addicts Anonymous, and, my personal favorite, Emotions Anonymous.

Matthew said to me, "Sometimes I get so sick of all this health."

I asked him if he wasn't grateful to be alive, didn't he want to live and be well. Standard party line, but sometimes it's all there is to work with.

"I am sometimes," he said. "But sometimes I'm not. Sometimes I have no gratitude at all."

I liked hearing that. That first six months, there were an awful lot of people I met who talked the talk, all the time. Their faces seemed to glow, and they'd go on about so-and-so "getting it," "getting" the program, having that much-touted aura of serenity about them. It was my experience that such persons usually relapsed and stole their roommate's stereo equipment, or charged five thousand dollars' worth of lingerie at Dayton's. Nobody gives up an addiction that easily, or it wouldn't be an addiction, just a problem. But it was easy to talk the talk. Everyone praised you and loved you to pieces if you could talk the talk. So Matthew's bleak words did not make me, as they say, "concerned." I just thought that in his own way he was braver than a lot of us and saying what we all were thinking. Besides, if there was anybody who tried to work those Twelve Simple Steps for Complicated People it was him.

That might have been one of the reasons I didn't get too concerned about his sex-addiction thing—pornography and prostitutes. I just didn't think the boy needed another Twelve-Step Program, and, to be honest, I refused to see what was so terrible about it. I just thought it was sad and creepy, but my frame of reference, when it came to men, told me that most men were, at heart, sad and creepy. He didn't beat the women up, he didn't harm them, so what was the need for yet another Anonymous group? Anyway, some men were just born to be customers: that's what a friend of mine, a former working girl, told me when I mentioned it. She is very tough, that woman is, the way I've always wanted to be.

The truth is, I thought it was funny when I found the stack of magazines in his bathroom. They were a little on the severe side, with piston shots and all the rest of it, but not the worst I'd ever seen. When I first got out of the House, I'd worked in a bookstore that had an adult section. At first, when I was sorting the magazines for stacking, I had looked at the glossy pictures, but they quickly grew boring; not a lot interested me in those early days except thinking about drugs. Certainly not sex, except as a possible means for procuring drugs, in case I decided to relapse. Matthew, though, when he realized he'd forgotten to remove the magazines from the bathroom, acted as if I'd found some kind of forensic evidence. The color went right out of his face, and I could see what he looked like when he was thinking up a lie. "They're my roommate's," he said.

It didn't seem like a big deal to me. But I went back in there before I left, and surreptitiously checked the dates: the magazines were all new, the very latest. There was about five hundred dollars' worth of pornography stacked up in his pink-tiled bathroom. Just one month's supply. When I mentioned it to his roommate, he said, "You should get a load of his video collection."

Matthew went to Sex Addicts Anonymous on Tuesday nights, but, as I recall, he never managed more than a month of abstinence. I tried to talk Twelve-Step with him. I tried it while we were laughing about something else, so I wouldn't sound fatuous: "Look, every time you pay some little hooker on University Avenue you're enabling an addict. I mean maybe there are some prostitutes who aren't chemically dependent, but no street-level tootsie—which, let's face it, is

all you can afford—is out there for any other reason. You should be taking those girls to meetings."

I was not exactly on the mark with that one. Matthew didn't see them as addicts in need of recovery; he didn't see them at all. He told me it was just a thing he couldn't stop doing. "It seems like I get something out of making myself disgusting to myself. I mean, while I'm doing it, it feels good." I knew all about that, most certainly. "But you know me," he said. "You know that in real life I respect people." I knew about that, too—the loathsome thing about yourself that you refuse to let into your real life, because it isn't you, it isn't you at all.

I decided I didn't need to know about it. He didn't need to know everything about me, either. Your friends do not need to know everything about you. For instance, when my office pals would pick me up outside the Ramsey Medical Center on certain mornings to take me to work and save me an hour on the bus, I felt fine about just telling them I was seeing a dentist. Sometimes I was afraid that my prescription would fall out of my pocket and they'd recognize the name. That little drug is one medicine that gets a lot of press. It is the star, the celebrity, the Marilyn of medicines, so I made sure to keep its label tucked safely down in the lint-lined caverns of my old tweed coat.

Matthew, especially, I didn't feel like telling. When he asked me why I'd stopped seeing this or that boy, I gave him sardonic Twelve-Step jargon. "I didn't want to defocus off my own issues?" I said, lilting upward at the end of my sentence, imitating the passive-aggressive vocal patterns of a Minnesota treatment person. By inflecting your sentence as though it were a question you force the other person, rather than yourself, to take some kind

of a stand. They can agree or disagree; you're merely asking questions. It's a somewhat manipulative manner of dialogue?

And that should go on my list—that I wish I'd told Matthew I was not at the dentist's.

Telling Matthew might not have made a difference to what he eventually did, but it would have made a difference to me. I like to see myself as someone who is honest and loyal to her friends, even if she sometimes lies to them. Matthew thought I was, which is why he didn't mind saying what he said that day in his van.

"What woman," he asked, "would go with me if I didn't pay her?"

We were listening to Matthew's latest tape. It was a collection of new folk-music bands. The vocalists were all women with gentle, quavering voices.

"That's ridiculous," I told him. "You're kind, you're decent, you've got a job, andyou're very smart. Any woman would be proud to call you sweetie."

But that evening he came around to see if I could walk the walk as well as talk the talk. He'd bought a new sweater, and although it looked a bit like the sweaters his mother used to send him, it was a sweater that showed some daring. His mother's taste ran to pastels, with corporate-looking patterns worked into the textiles. This sweater was only one color, red, and it was made of some kind of yarn that did not look entirely synthetic.

I gave his shoulder a punch and said, "Come *on*. What *is* this?" Oh, I was getting good at Minnesota hide-and-seek. I knew exactly what he was doing.

"I want to take you out," he said, and his eyes rested on me, so pale-blue that they seemed gray. I felt that I was looking pale myself. I felt my old revulsion start up, the desire to keep on playing with the puppets and not hear what was being said.

"Matthew, I'm not sure that's a good idea? We have a very valuable friendship?"

"That's why it's a good idea. We've both been sober a year, and neither of us has been in what you could call a 'relationship.' So we could just, you know, just try it . . . Unless—" He didn't finish the unless, but I could have finished it for him: "Unless you were lying. Unless I really am disgusting to your eyes and the eyes of women."

I was having trouble—I *am* having trouble—thinking of myself as a "woman." Anyhow, I had plenty of reasons not to step out in a serious manner, with him or with anyone. The problem was that I didn't want to think about any of these particular reasons. I didn't want to think about the fact that I wasn't in tip-top relationship shape. I didn't want to tell him about my health status. There are some things that I Would Never tell anyone, and I didn't want to tell my friend Matthew anything at all. He was holding the flowers, and I could see them trembling gently, as if touched by a small draft.

"Matthew," I said, "it's probably not real sober behavior for me to start dating perverts."

Not that we never spoke to each other again, or anything so efficient, so tidy, as all that. I passed it off as a joke; he passed it off as passing insanity. But we didn't meet at lunchtime anymore, and if we talked on the phone one of us always

had to hang up and do something pressing. Usually he was going to some kind of Meeting. He was starting to go to more and more different kinds. He was very excited about one called No More Shame. I'd gone back to school, and I was making a lot of noise about how when you start living an actual life you don't have time to just endlessly hang out with people anymore.

It was the next spring when I last talked to Matthew on the telephone. He told me he was leaving to go set up a new line for InfoSystem in a city in Indonesia. I reminded him that Southeast Asia was where they manufactured his drug of choice, but he didn't seem concerned. I didn't press it; I hate to sound like some AA Aunt Nellie. Besides, I could tell from his hushed, gravelly-sounding voice that he had already slipped out of our little recovery community. Which is just something that happens: people come, they go, they leave town. Sometimes they come back, sometimes not. If I were a lounge singer, I'd name it "A Little Process Called Life."

Matthew's parents came to Minnesota from Sault Ste. Marie a few months after he'd left. They said they needed to straighten out some business, but I think they just wanted to see the place that he had told them about, back when he was telling them things. For three months, he hadn't told them, or anyone else, anything; he had asked them to take out some of his savings and send him a Western Union money order in June—and then nothing. They sat across from me at the coffee shop with their backs straight and their hands under the table. His father was wearing a sweater that had

clearly been purchased by his wife. On his father it did not look at all out of place. He was a man with huge, bony hands—knuckles and sinew, planklike wrists. He said, "Matthew told us you and he liked to listen to music together. He loves music. I always thought he had interesting taste. Very sophisticated."

"Jim and I have been praying," his mother said. "Not for any results, but just for acceptance."

"And for Matthew to get well," his father added. "For Matthew to find some peace." I didn't point out the contradiction between this and his wife's "acceptance" remark. Instead, I tried to smile, as if we all knew the same prayers, and I kept looking at Matthew's father, who had put his arm behind his wife's shoulders. If Matthew ever came back, he would fit into his father's sweaters in about twenty years. Every time the shop door opened I shivered a little; the breeze went right through the chiffon blouse I was wearing. It was see-through, so I wore a tank top under it, insouciant and very fashionable. I'd seen it on all sorts of beautiful young girls, in restaurants and coffee shops all over town.

I seem to have trouble sticking to the list idea; my counselor would probably tell me to get some distance from it, go take a walk in the sun. Well, the sun is good for you only in small doses, but I'm making my peace with it. I no longer plot my walk to work exclusively along streets I know will be in the shade. I even sit on my porch in the daytime; it's a good porch, because it gets just a little sun, about twenty minutes in the late afternoon. Which is when the kids from next

door come over to swing on my hammock and ask me questions. There are six of them, I think, but they seem like more because I can't keep their names straight. Their names are Cambodian, and I can't pronounce them. They're from the same region as Matthew's drug of choice, and mine, and yet they have come here; that should tell me something. I wish I were better at saying their names, but it's pretty clear at this point that I don't have much of an ear for language, and I can put that on the list: I Will Never learn to speak another language. It's not important, in this case, since these kids speak English, which is sometimes a bad thing, depending on what they have to tell me. For instance, when the oldest girl told me that she used to have a baby brother but a soldier swung him into a tree and cracked his head, I would have been perfectly happy if she hadn't known how to tell me this. All I could find to say was, "Are you sure?" She might have been making it up to get me to give her more crackers and jelly.

"Sure," she says. "That day, it was rain." But she's only thirteen years old, so maybe she won't have to keep seeing that picture at night, when her eyes are shut and she's trying to focus on positive, relaxing images, the way she'll surely learn to do—this being America, after all.

Her ten-year-old sister is too young to remember anything like that, but she enjoys punching people in the arm. A painful and annoying habit, but at least it usually distracts her from snooping around inside my house. Last week, she and the two boys came running out of my kitchen brandishing a half-empty container of AZT.

"Why you take medicine?" they shouted. "Are you sick?"

"Stay out of my kitchen!" I shouted back, making a grab for my tablets. "No. They're like vitamins. I take them so I won't get sick."

The girl, obviously the ringleader of the kitchen-snooping expedition, punched me in the arm. "You won't get sick," she said. "You're strong. You just have to let me punch you in the arm every day, and you won't get sick." I wish that were true. I'd still rather get punched in the arm every day than take drugs that don't get me high. It's unnatural as a concept, and frightening in its implication. And what if I have to put that, finally, on my list: I Will Never get high again.

Matthew probably had something like that on his list—something with the word "never" in it. It's no good to think like that, in such grandiose and sweeping language. I could have told him. It may be jargon, but it's true. It's better not to think in these agonized, religious extremes. Better to just break it down into smaller, more manageable units of time. The nice thing about small units of time is how they add up. I've added them up, so far, into two years, three months, four days, and right up into this minute, right now, on my porch, where I am watching these children play the parachute game, which is their favorite game because it involves an unlimited amount of shrieking, yelling, kicking, and bossing each other around.

It's a simple game. One by one, the kids crawl under the parachute, and I twist them up inside it. I roll them around and drape the fabric over them in labyrinthine folds until all that can be seen is a big pile of red silk, full of squealing

lumps, and then I say, "Go!" The game is to get out while accidentally clocking as many of your brothers and sisters on the jaw as you possibly can. The silk never rips: it's designed to take on the wind in the sky; there's no chance a little kid is going to put a sneaker through it. When one emerges, he or she stands there yelling instructions to the ones still inside. "The other way, kick with your legs." As they begin to tumble out, they start to count: "That's two of us . . . That's four . . ." But the sixth and last, a tiny girl of three, can't find her way out. We can hear a thin, terrified wail coming from deep inside the red silk folds. The oldest girl, with a slight, hissing breath, goes to the parachute and unfolds it with quick, flinging motions, as if she were making a bed. In three seconds, the sixth and littlest is out, standing upright, silent, an embarrassed smile on her face, sparkling quietly like a candied plum.

MY BIG RED HEART

On St. Valentine's Day in St. Paul, Minnesota, I put the bills I was paying onto the kitchen table, threw on my snow boots, and bundled off into the sparkling blue arctic street, heading for the coffee shop in order to play board games with other sorry humans. Everything was in alignment—I was tired, confused, anemic, and angst-ridden; when someone made a joke, my laughter was high and shattery. Walking around in a state of near-total disorientation with a toddler's eagerness to please, I was pretty sure I was going to get lucky. I'm nothing but a walking boy magnet when my guard is down like that, an apple-cheeked six-year-old with breasts singing, "Daddy, daddy, tie my shoe." Sure enough into that chattering adolescent-infested caffeine haven came my friend with a friend of his friend. Introductions were made and I noticed my friend's friend had bicolored eyes. One green and one blue. Rich emerald green for "go" and pale frozen blue for "stop right there, sister." Very talkative eyes, flashing out a blinking story told in beginner's code:

"I can hardly speak," his eyes said. "I don't know what to say.

My soul is a jungle at nightfall. I don't like to play Scrabble or Monopoly. I don't know what I like. I like looking at you. I smoked so much pot in high school that even now, fifteen years later, whole weeks go by and I can't make a sound. I once knew a girl who looked like you, her hair was soft as black smoke, her mouth a burning rose, but I married the next girl, a certified public accountant with a straw-colored headband. She left me, finally. I don't know if I miss her. She's coming back to me tomorrow on the five-fifteen and I'll wait in the hills by the station howling her sad, sad name. Sadder still, I'll forget to pick her up, having gotten involved in a conversation about Engels, whose book I have read the blurbs on, and I'll lose track of the time. I'm confused, I'm disoriented, somebody help me. You. You help me. Help me with your breasts and hips and sweet, sweet pussy stronger than a thousand sacred vows of justice."

I sat there, staring right back at him, my hands shaking from the second double latté. I tried to listen to that soft, still voice within, but as usual it was too busy screaming "run" to tell me anything I needed to know. My fluttering fingers beat out a "maybe yes, maybe no" on the Formica countertop. He poured a packet of sugar into his coffee, stirred it up, and talked some more to see how good a listener I was. His eyes became strobe lights, flashing in time with the arrhythmia in my chest. "Hey, honey-snack," said those blue and green eyes, "do you know the people you see walking around pained and in a daze as if they've just walked into a wall and scraped their foreheads? All former friends of mine who didn't understand that it was time to move on. I have to keep moving, I'm on a quest. I haven't decided yet whether I'm going for worldly success or spiritual

glory, but the sorry truth is you can't make an omelet without breaking eggs. Some of my favorite eggs include:

"My mother's heart.

"My best friend's marriage.

"The peace of mind of anyone who's ever kissed my dry, hot mouth.

"The peace of mind of anyone who's ever stood next to me in the checkout line at Rainbow Foods.

"The economic stability of emerging nations that I passed through on spring break."

With every single sip of New Guinea Dark, he was just getting cuter and cuter, singing that age-old song I always love to hear.

"It's true," his eyes went on as he lit my cigarette, "I used my last girlfriend's flesh in an upholstery experiment, but she assured me, swore up and down that she didn't need skin. Her eyes were wide open, she knew what she was getting into. But I don't need to tell you that, I know you know you're different. I'd never rip off such beautiful soft porcelain skin. You I would cherish. You I would idolize. You I would make the queen of my better nature. Just because I have, in the past, made women into furniture doesn't mean you're not safe with me, and I may not know much, darlin', but I do know this: There is no man anywhere so psychotic, so drunk, so evil, so helpless, so brutal, indifferent, or even just annoying that some woman some-where won't keep him warm even if she freezes to death doing it, just for a chance to wipe away the invisible tears she thinks she sees on his face, like clear ice on a cold windowpane."

I could feel it happening, the room starting to swoop around; that empty feeling in my stomach like I was looking

down into a long drop. He touched my elbow when I stood up and I sat back down, a dog for tenderness.

"Here's the straight-up verity," his eyes said, going all gangster-beatnik. "There is nothing that I pass by that I leave untouched. I'm quiet, but I'm hungry. I absorb things like an amoeba, and I have its calm clearness of purpose. I'm going to tell you the truth so you can't say you weren't warned. I'm a human car accident. I'm what it looks like after a train wreck. I'm a ship going down into the icy, black North Atlantic. I'm a Molotov cocktail in an Alzheimered fist. I'm the dictionary definition of sadness. Baby," his eyes beamed at me, "I'm your man."

Maybe, I thought, I'll take a cue from the world of kitty-cats: rub up against his ankles while looking off elsewhere, and then be on my way. Or possibly, I thought, as the walls spun and the greasy seasick floor lurched in the fluorescent lamplight, this is Real Love at long last. But in the end I went to the bathroom and snuck out the back door.

4

At the hour in the middle of the night when there is nothing moving, your digital clock radio will come on all at once, for no other reason than it's as you've always suspected: inanimate objects aren't inanimate at all, but are instead possessed of soul and will, and mean you no good. At first it will sound far away, tinny-soft and static, like an orange-and-yellow merengue floating out from behind corrugated bodega awnings, or like a memory of listening to music in a Jersey seaside town with its striped revival tents, stone canals, and long-gone-from-high-school students manning the arcades by the Atlantic with their shag haircuts and pebble-gray eyes. Then the sound will become audibly swollen, and even though you try to switch the dial, switch it off, yank the plug, let the gadget sail clacking and clattering into the wall, its chatter won't stop, but instead only grows more persistent until you can discern different elements, different voices, all saying things you don't want to hear, and this, my darling, is RadioDeath, this is Radio Fear, coming to you straight and true and live over the airtight, airless waves of longing, and we are playing all the hits tonight:

The voice of that person you loved and left singing in small chanting words a child's song, you remember that one; and the conspicuous absence of laughter after that last misplaced joke you tried to tell at your uncle's wake, your uncle whom nobody liked but didn't really want to hear jokes about; we are replaying that two seconds of silence in the mix forever and ever; and the sound of the counselor at the resort your parents took you to announcing your win in the swimming race, the win you had cheated for by pushing off with your feet, more running than swimming; your fake panting, the sound of your desire to win, and your fake panting sounds when you were doing the ding-dong with that boy you met or that girl you met at that bar or that AA meeting who you didn't know well enough to talk to about your genitals and so you just pretended to be swept up in the moment, that cry of faux pleasure will echo like a dial tone all night on this all-night station, don't turn over, darling, I'm right here, I'm right here like an eternal mosquito coming to you on a frequency of megawatts too large for you to even conceive of, and I'm never leaving you again, this is all-night good-time radio—you'll never have to be alone in the dark the way I was, but it turned out it wasn't such a good idea to leave me alone with no lights on because now we're going to replay, again and again, my fear of the dark, except it will be yours now and there's no getting out of it ever, no getting up to turn on the light, there will be no light ever again, except from the green dashboard-glow of the digital clock which will never change to the next minute and no sound either except the sound of my voice replaying over and over again

the litany of times that you failed, or might fail, or might have failed without knowing it. Call me a prick if you like. The prick of conscience. Oh, relax my own sweet country 'tis of thee till dawn's early light, this is me on the radio, and I'm coming to get you, coming to you, coming to you live.

GLAMOUR GIRL

It may seem, by now, that males have always had incredible power over me, even more than over the average PWV, which stands for Person With A Vagina, the first of many acronyms in an initial-cluttered life. At one point, one of the dozens of therapeutic professionals I have had the chance to meet with advised me to find the "Red Thread" running through my history, the one thing that twined through it constantly. Unknot this ball of muddy yarn and you will find it threaded with the thin, mean little filaments of acronyms. Another is made up of men.

From nursery school on, I craved their love and approval in the way I would later come to crave alcohol, cocaine, and opiates. "Glory," said my mother, "is going to grow up to be a lover of men." In this I would only be following her unspoken but clearly-voiced example.

She was the definition of languid, lying prostrate on the couch, her hands dangling over the edge like pale, broken butterflies that had fluttered down to their last resting place. I was three or four years old, and she was sobbing because her

husband, my biological father, had not come to visit when he had promised, *promised*, that he would. The whole scene was like a Maxfield Parrish painting: the overwrought, pale bronze light of late afternoon illuminating the dark, Park Avenue living room like a shower of Zeus's golden coins, my mother a swan-maiden in diaphanous, artfully draped fabric, brought down by an unseen arrow. Forget the terry cloth bathrobe she was actually wearing and edit out the sixty-year-old African American housekeeper who was sorting our laundry in the kitchen. "Daddy loves us though," I said, in the wise voice of toddlers parroting the homilies of their parents. My mother raised her head from the arms of the couch. "No," she said, "he doesn't."

This news caused an ontological gash in the fabric of my conscious reality: husbands not love wives? Parents not love children? If this could be, then they could forget about telling me it was just as safe to sleep in the dark as with the lights on.

To be fair, my mother got up off the chaise lounge, went back to school to get her master's degree, and got me a new father—a doctor. A short, wiry, old-school tough guy, with a bantam-rooster walk and a love of classical music, he still carried a faint trace of Depression-era Brooklyn in his voice, which surfaced only when he got angry. He adored his new wife the same way he adored Chopin—fiercely and without reason. And who wouldn't adore her, the doe-eyed, sensitive, feminist, gentle-voiced vision of an America without harsh-toned women cutting coupons in poorly-lit Flatbush Avenue kitchens? Who wouldn't love a woman with a mouth

like a lush gardenia who could ask her housekeeper to have dinner ready at six so she could attend an afternoon peace march in Central Park? Who wouldn't love a woman who believed in Sigmund Freud the way a Catholic laundress believes in the Holy Mother?

But his new daughter seemed to have something wrong with her brain: She needed to be the center of attention all the time; she couldn't complete the simplest task; she lied, fought, showed off, and, at an age when most girls couldn't stand them, she chased boys. She also spilled things and knocked things over, which made him slam his fist onto the dining room table. The fact was, however, that he loved her, too, and not only because her eyes were the same color as her mother's.

What I learned from my mother's devotion to this man was simple—requited love is boring, but necessary. And you are nothing, nothing, nothing, without a man, or, to put it simply, you have no Glamour without one. This lesson is not something my mother would have ever imparted verbally, in fact, it may not have been something she imparted at all. It may have been simply the way I assembled the story from a frightened child's way with facts. Nonetheless, for all her elaborate bouquets of wealthy-hippie verbal foliage, I thought this was what she believed in the dark room where she kept her unspeakable truths.

So, without boys, I knew I would be condemned to an eternity without Glamour. And who—this is the lesson that my mother did speak out loud—craved Glamour? Bad people, doomed by their badness to a permanently

Glamourless hell. Glamour, after all, originally meant a spell cast by faeries, that made everything seem beautiful. Propitiating these unseen and powerful forces was only prudent—but it was also savage and cowardly.

The truth, in fact, was that I didn't much like men. I didn't dislike them, but as individuals they were no more relevant than any other item in the cold, bright storage space of my waking life. I simply needed what their affection would bestow upon me—the light of existence.

In other words, I hated boys because they had so much power over me: I wanted them to love me. And I wanted them to love me because without their love I had no power. If boys didn't like me, no one would. To hell with them. I'd have to make them like me. A line of reasoning as tangled as any knotted piece of thread could get. But Glamour was an evil faerie that sunk its meathooks into my tiny chest and pulled me around for the next thirty years, and boys were Glamorous.

My need for this certain kind of Glamour, let's call it love, flourished like something in a dark refrigerator until it became something almost separate from myself, a monster I had no memory of creating.

In the meantime, I was compelled to elicit alarm and repulsion wherever I walked. In junior high, this became a problem. Not that boys, even in the seventies, didn't have absolute and irrefutable power over other girls besides me, I just had a noisier way of dealing with it than most.

I also had what now might be called Attention Deficit Disorder, ADD by acronym. I couldn't find my socks half the

time, and the rest of the time they were mismatched. I couldn't brush my hair, bathe regularly, sit still, or keep my mouth shut. I negotiated social situations with inappropriate jokes delivered in the same loud, game-showy voice I had heard men use. I hadn't heard many women tell jokes, and the ones that did were all ugly, which was mainly what they told their jokes about.

"You're a remarkable little girl," said my beautiful, doe-eyed feminist mother, "and you're lucky, because if you conquer all your enormous problems, there's nothing in the world you can't become." These twilight feminist cooings were quickly drowned out by reality's sonic boom.

PANTY RAIDER

When I was twelve, I was sent to boarding school because I had flunked, failed, and truanced myself out of all the decent private schools my parents had tried to keep me in. There, I was compelled to hurl the squeaky little song of myself into that very sonic boom. On the second day, in the common room, I noticed a clique of the cool kids. You knew they were the cool kids because you just knew—maybe they were the best-looking or maybe they just seemed like it because of the aura of dominant charisma that hovered around their table like a tangible, magnetic phenomenon. The faeries had done their work on them—perhaps using nothing but genetics to cast the spell. They glowed and hummed with a force that both attracted and repelled.

Fresh from the city, I was wearing the watered-down flower-child garb my mother and I both liked: clogs, peasant skirts,

and Maria Muldaur hair—long, with frizzy waves rolling down to the middle of my back. This was all fine for the Upper West Side, but I was in Connecticut; these kids had all attended this school as day students since the first grade, and there had been no sartorial change in these people's consciousness since 1962.

The girls, all blonde with hair as straight and gleaming as gilt paper, wore corduroy skirts and argyle knee socks. They, too, understood the notion of a single thread: at all times there must be a thread of color in the pattern of their argyles that matched the color of the turtleneck peaking out from under their sweater; this was the secret sign that let you breathe the wintergreen air with your head held high. The boys had completely flat asses and blue eyes. I wanted desperately for them all to love me, which, of course, made me hate them.

And so I came crashing right down in their midst and began to talk loudly while chewing with my mouth open. This spectacle was compounded by the fact that I did not wear a bra and I was starting to get breasts, a development which my mother assured me was a beautiful and natural process. It took two days for everyone to start calling me "Tits" and declare me a Loud-Mouthed Ugly Slut Who Would Suck Your Dick For A Quarter. My hair, which they called a JewFro, gained me the nickname "Bride of Frankenstein." When we were given the actual book itself in second-semester English, I had to force myself to read it. In class discussion I defended the monster's actions, and, naturally, the laughter was as loud as I had expected it would be.

I won't say my feelings weren't hurt, but there was a part of me that reveled in the opprobrium. Who wouldn't? Each day brought a new challenge. Would I be chased by a group of

second-string eighth-grade soccer players who would throw me down and pretend to hump my back? Would my chair be pulled out from under me as I attempted to take a seat in Ancient History? I wanted to be the belle of the ball, and in a strange way I was. There was always the enthralling, episodic battle between myself and the good, natural world which I horrified and infuriated. As long as the villagers kept coming after me with their torches, my life was a torchlight parade.

I saw myself, heroically, like the monster driven out from the ringleted Swiss family to whom he secretly became attached. He wanted them to like him, and they did not. Party-crasher, Banquo's ghost, I took my revenge by inflicting myself upon them: Nothing, but nothing, could make me shut my big mouth.

Each morning I would resolve to make it through the day without speaking, thereby avoiding misery. Ugly girls were supposed to remain in the background and I swore to myself with all my heart that I'd comply. I would keep my hand down. I would keep my mouth closed. Each day, however, I would say something loud, nasty, and certifiably sure to draw taunts and insults down onto my frizzy head.

No one appreciated my devastating wit except for one boy who had in the meantime transferred to another school. He wrote me long, self-revelatory love letters. I was encouraged to respond to him by the girls in my dorm: "He plays varsity," they said.

He had the flat ass and the blue eyes, and he even had the beautifully burnished first name of Bennett. For a while, he seemed to be the ticket to the endless Elysian Prom that

everyone else was going to attend. But there was something a little unnerving about him, something that even I, who wanted to walk in the kind of sunlight that only a boyfriend could grant me, found daunting. His letters careened out of control. "You are a free spirit," he wrote me, "someone who doesn't bow down to convention. This is a rare and beautiful thing. You must have gotten that from your mother. She is brave and beautiful like you are. I still remember her in her long, flowing peasant skirt at the Parents' Day ceremony, sitting on the grass. Glory, I knew she wasn't wearing any underpants." And so on.

He liked to tell me how much he disliked himself, how he'd bought boots because he couldn't tie his shoes but then he tripped over them. Just when he'd gotten my sympathy he'd also mention that his latest sexual cartoon fantasy was to insert a bicycle pump into a redheaded centerfold and pump it until she blew up like an overinflated tire. "I told my mother about it, and she just laughed at me," he wrote, "but she laughs at anything after her third gin & tonic, and then pretends she never heard it." His mother, a tall woman with red-splashed cheeks, a hardy stride, and a nickering laugh, had an administrative position in the headmaster's office. "Just to keep me honest Injun," she would chortle, as if slightly embarrassed to have a job.

I finally decided that I didn't want to hear from him anymore, even though his letters upped my Glamour quotient considerably.

Bennett, before he had left, had been a fairly popular piece of work: not an Alpha, but not one of the usual Omega freaks

to which I had usually been reduced to running. The fact that he liked me and I was publicly unsure whether I liked him back gave me just a little of that thing I hated myself for craving. I wanted more of it. My newfound status as someone's object of desire, plus my vociferous academic and behavioral failings (I was constantly being called up in front of the assembled student body for some infraction or another) gave me a certain transgressive panache in the eyes of my peers. Some of the coolest kids began to allow me to tag along on their midnight pot-smoking, Zeppelin-listening, finger-fucking expeditions.

One night, right after spring break, they were caught bending over the bong, boys in a girl's room, after curfew. If boys got caught in a girl's dorm, the girls got suspended. If girls got caught in a boy's dorm . . . the girls got suspended. This, said the headmaster, was to encourage chivalry on the part of the boys. But if anybody, of any gender, race, creed, or color, got caught smoking pot, it meant immediate expulsion. Unless you were an integral part of that year's varsity lacrosse team, which was the recipient of much alumni generosity, in the form of checks spotted with a nostalgic, manly tear or two.

I was overlooked during the roundup, since I was in the bathroom at the time, trying to talk myself out of an intense episode of paranoia. "You *won't* forget how to breathe," I said earnestly to the mirror.

Every single student they found, they expelled.

Immediately the miscreants were canonized in graffiti on bathroom walls and bulletin boards. They acquired the glow of antiauthoritarian martyrs to the Cause. Which Cause,

exactly, was up for question, but the gleam around their names was indisputable. I wanted in. I wanted in so much that I marched into the headmaster's office to confess my crimes and be expelled.

While waiting outside his office, however, I remembered the last time I had come home with bad news. I had gone on a skiing trip and lost, *lost*, the expensive Rossignols my parents had bought me. During the taxi ride home from the airport my mother's eyes had turned into venomous slits as she kept up a hissing monologue between clenched teeth about how selfish I was, how destructive, spoiled, uncaring, hateful, vile, and generally disappointing. "I had such hopes for you when you were born. I guess it's God's little joke on me that you turned out to be the sorrow of my life. You clearly despise us . . . all the money we've spent on you, you'd take it and use it for toilet paper if you could . . . Do you have any idea how many thousands of dollars we've already spent that you've wiped your ass with?"

And so on. Into the house and through the living room into the kitchen. Until she heard the lock in the door downstairs turn and my father's step on the landing. At which point she changed gears with more speed and grace than a million-dollar racecar and sank, fluttered really, in her ersatz gypsy-pattern damsel-in-distress outfit, into the chair and began sobbing helplessly—a woman abused and berated beyond all endurance. My father ran at me like a rottweiler. "What the hell have you been doing to your mother, you rotten little bitch?" And I felt her eyes on me, triumphant, as he

chased me up the stairs and into my room—this was what you could get men to do for you if you played them like the instruments they were.

Even then I saw no way to avoid repeating this scene in different permutations throughout my life, but I honestly thought that a fresh disappointment of this magnitude, expulsion from the last place they could find to put me in, would result in some kind of permanent exile from what was left of their affections. And their affection was everything to me. After all, these were the same people who had read me installments of *The Little Prince* after dinner every night, tears pooling behind my stepfather's glasses as we got to the last chapter. They would certainly kick me out of the house.

So while I did go into the headmaster's office and admit to smoking pot with the other kids, I modified the time frame a little bit. I said I had done it in January, three months prior. I was spared the expulsion and granted the sainthood: having tragically announced to the assembled students in the butt room that for the sake of my own clear conscience I was going to confess. I couldn't let my friends go down without me.

There are things in life that can't always be explained: No one was in the headmaster's office except for the headmaster, the dean of students, and myself. Certainly Bennett's mother was in the outer office, laughing on the phone with someone from her club, but everything said in the confines of the headmaster's office, I was repeatedly assured, was confidential. So why, when I called on the counselors at the prep school of the still-persisting Bennett to stop him from writing to me did I get an apologetic phone call from him, almost squirmingly

contrite, but with his usual undertone of freaky menace? "I heard a nasty rumor," he said, "of course I don't believe it. I heard you were actually in that office confessing to things you did *last semester*. My mother has some things she says can prove it, but you can't always trust your mother."

Of course I denied it. Then came more apologetic wriggling from him, along with the request for a souvenir. A memento. A lock of my hair in the mail. Better yet, a pair of my underpants.

Assuming that, unlike my mother, I wore any.

Not clean underpants; he wanted PSP, that's what the other guys at the school called what their girlfriends sent them: Pussy-Stained Panties.

Fear is a great motivator. Ordinarily the task of finding an envelope, finding a pen to write the address with, finding the address, putting the contents in the envelope, finding a stamp, and remembering to put the whole thing into the mailbox would have been too overwhelming and exhausting even to visualize. But I knew what the stakes were: total social annihilation.

Which was what my cowardly, craven little heart deserved.

But I didn't want to get what I deserved. Who does?

So, not just once, but every so often, it was PSP in the U.S. Mail to Bennett and the boys.

PUNK ROCK RULES

Eventually I was expelled from boarding school for bad grades, fighting, and general disastrousness. My parents sent me to a school in the city for Gifted Underachievers, called GAs, and once there I began to blossom. All the kids there were crazy,

and all of them were acting out. There were no cool kids, no sports teams, no theater groups, nor even any homework. There was no way to define success or failure. If you didn't overdose on Tuinols or throw a desk out the window during lunch you were defined, for that day at least, as progressing well. It was, however, in New York City, which meant that nothing you could do could compare to the city itself. I began to develop a peer group that found my company tolerable, and, soon enough, around 1979, after it had already fizzled, of course, we found punk rock.

I had no illusions that punk was going to offer me sanctuary. The rules of behavior, dress, and affect were as rigid as anything that had cohered over the eons at any prep school. Still, I thought there might be a place for me at the table. Of course I went about it in my own way. I wore my punk clothes around the house where they would be sure to offend and upset my family. Downtown, however, I always seemed to find myself in my preppy cashmere sweater and baggy corduroys. It was as if I were possessed by some kind of Anti-Glamour demon that compelled me, against my will, to break the rules of whatever circle I found myself in. A malevolent dybbuk had attached itself to me, its mission in the universe to make sure I did things to make myself unpopular. If preppy schlep-wear failed to annoy, I wore spandex bridge-and-tunnel disco outfits. My mother said that I was disguising myself as a member of the working class in order to denigrate everything she and our culture stood for. It also garnered me glares and stares from the East Village art students who were working on developing their heroin habits and cockney accents.

I got spit on at a few of the downtown clubs, in that brief era when spitting was a trendy homage to the Sex Pistols. My mother would sometimes just look at me and let her eyes fill with tears.

Things were going well.

I saw the future opening up before me; I could feel the dark stirrings of something momentous coming to life.

One night, two days after my eighteenth birthday, I was downtown at CBGB's when my friends started whispering. There was some local celebrity in the club. He was an underground writer, a scenester whose acerbic, pyrotechnic verbiage was the written equivalent of the sound of the moment. I was wearing my purple-satin, camel-toe pants and a red leather jacket, and I was drinking brown liquor, for which I was developing something more than a fondness. They pointed this guy out. He was archetypal New York early-eighties material: thin, with a complexion like dirty white paper and a snarl plastered on his face. Deference showed in the shrugs and shuffles of his entourage. I desperately wanted to climb the social ladder of this Brave New World and there he stood, at the top, holding all the tickets. Who the hell did he think he was? Was he any better than me? Was he smarter, more talented? No. Would he think I was pretty? Would he notice me at all? Would he understand the subtly transgressive irony of my purple disco pants? Why, again, was I wearing purple disco pants to a place where only black was allowed? To punish myself and those around me for my own disgusting need to be liked, of course. I felt like smashing a beer bottle over someone's head. Better yet, over my own.

So I walked up to him, another one of my expert breeches in protocol, and said something right to his face that I thought would impress him, something daring and clever like "Disco Rules," or something equally calculated to endear me to my context. He stood back and almost reeled from the outlandishness of being approached by one of the entry-fee-paying rabble. "That person," he said in a loud, sonorous voice that cut right through the three-chord stomp being laid down by the band, "that person there is an asshole."

Bouncers came by to see what had disturbed one of their favored patrons. He pointed at me and they surrounded me on either side, softly at first, like two inky-black clouds of leather. Then I was ejected, but not without a fight. They had to drag me out of there hollering. My tailbone hit the pavement hard, with a not-entirely-unpleasant sensation of cracking on concrete. "You're lucky you're a girl," said the bigger one, "or I'd kick your fucking ribs in."

"Go ahead," I screamed, "Kick my fucking ribs in!" But they'd vanished inside, leaving me sitting splay-legged on the Bowery, hollering curses. I was humiliated, and bitterly happy. Once again I had proven there were rules everywhere and I was capable of following exactly none of them, whether I wanted to or not.

BOYS OF THE WEST

In my early twenties, after failing out of college because of too much getting drunk and obsessing about various boys, I began to run around with a group of guys who rejected the facile posings of punk rock. Instead, they incessantly read Henry Miller.

At various times one or another of them professed his love for me. That's how I was, no Universal Femme Fatale, but capable, like caviar, of inspiring intense adoration in a few select unbalanced souls. They were devoted to the idea of me, a Free Spirit Without Underwear, a garment I had ceased to make use of the instant I was out of Bennett's blackmailing range.

Helpless under the spell of even possible admiration, I cherished my place in this little group. I carefully hid from them the fact that I was only fit for real monsters. One day the boys I tagged along with told me I drank too much and would drink less in Portland, Oregon, because it was a less spiritually corrupt place than New York.

Although I had no intention of drinking less, I went along because I was the only female character in this heroic tale of youthful iconoclasts, perched sassily somewhere between cohort and mascot. Need I tell you how much I relished that gleaming tomboy spotlight? Promptly, I whined busfare out of my parents and off I went, hot on the heels of whomever it was I had a big ol' crush on that particular week. I brought nothing with me except for a few changes of clothes and a battered copy of *Ice* by Anna Kavan. I lost it, the way I lost all objects that were not organically attached to my body. Fortunately there were a million used bookstores in that drizzle-spattered city, so I haunted them, looking for a replacement.

In the process, I wound up working at one of the taverns next door to an old occult bookshop, and before you could say "You're fired, Glory," I ended up married to the bartender. The bar had become the center of our little scene. Since all the

boys I had come out West with were drinkers (their judgment of my drinking habits a projection of their own), everyone we met was a drinker.

The tavern was called something nautical like The First Mate's Gristle or The Rusted Anchor, but it had been a long time since anyone in the sailing business had staggered in or out of its salmon-trimmed, periwinkle-blue-painted doors. Instead, it was home to a collection of stewardesses who practiced Wiccan magic; watercolorists who worked as carpenters; bearded, sandaled practitioners of New Age ballroom dance techniques; the occasional skinhead, poet, or disoriented punk rocker on their way to somewhere else; circus performers on leaves of absence; and a few stray wanna-be yuppies who kept missing the waves of prosperity that were rolling up so regularly in 1985.

What everyone had in common was that they were drunk most of the time. And coked up and snorting speed and gobbling Valium and falling asleep on each other's couches and walking around in each other's clothes.

Big man on this little campus, status symbol to be seen on the scene on his arm, was the boy to whom I was briefly married. We shared a fondness for alcohol, cocaine, and histrionic acts of self-destruction. He was the bartender, which, in our little world, made him quite the catch. He could dance, either on the floor or on the bar, and cast a mean glance or ignore a woman in the way a certain kind of woman can't resist.

A theater major and would-be writer, he loved me first and foremost for being a Jewish girl from New York. Yes, yes, I would tell him in the middle of the night while we drunkenly

fucked on some railroad tracks, eyeing each other to see who would get nervous first: Persian rugs on hardwood parquet floors, bookshelves lined with Aeschylus, Euripides, Einstein, Marx, Freud, Brecht, and Kierkegaard. I would have said anything, endured a million drunken diatribes on class consciousness and how I was basically a bourgeois princess while he was a heroic pauper, just so I could be seen with him, in that tavern, on a side street in a city somewhere in the Pacific Northwest, by people whose faces and names I can't even remember now.

I do remember that he cheated on me constantly, and I was obsessed with how bad that made me look. So I'd cheat on him, in between getting fired from various jobs for bookkeeping errors and tardiness. I'd find him in our bed with some girl when he thought I was still in the hospital with a kidney infection and break a plate over his head. He'd think I was screwing his best friend and black both my eyes. He'd leave me and walk down the block, righteous. I'd follow him, begging and pleading. I'd go back to New York, he would call and write and beg and plead. I would call and write and beg and plead with my poor mother to send me the airfare back out for another round. "Mom," I'd whine and badger, my voice a vicious squeak, "you have to or I'll die. Die. I mean it. Do you want me to die, you probably do, but give me the money anyhow." And so on. Whatever it took.

Naturally it was humiliating, but I choked it back, because nothing was more important than that I emerge victorious from the contest I thought I was in with this guy I was briefly

married to and the color of whose eyes I couldn't tell you now on a bet. When I finally went back home for good, the entire city of New York couldn't take my mind off the image of this guy back in Portland fucking everybody in this little tavern and being really popular. For four months after our last breakup I wandered around hollow-eyed like the Madwoman of Your Local Tower of Abandonment trying to figure out a way to get him back so I could break up with him and thus win the game I was forced to play, despite hooting derision from all my upper-brain functions.

I had dabbled, in my late teens and early twenties, in the art of Gender Vengeance, but at the age of twenty-four, I took it up in earnest. I made assignations and broke them, only to show up at our arranged meeting place on the arm of someone else. In whispered love-bouts I stared into the eyes of boys until I could detect a trace of openness and swore my love. Once I saw even a flicker of requital I would walk down the stairs for a pack of cigarettes and not come back.

One of them followed me down the street—a hardworking electrician who played the bass and, it's safe to say, had never hurt another living soul in the whole of his life. "Why would you do this to me?" he kept asking. For a brief moment, the quiet block of Bedford Avenue in Williamsburg glowed with my triumph. The universe was becoming a golden antithesis of itself—it was a place where I did the walking and all manner of things stumbled after me, crippled with yearning. But what did this cosmic heartbreaker do then? Oh, she went home and sobbed with guilt. How could she do that to anyone? Imagine the Blue Angel

herself—her parched, affectless monotone gone high and keening—on the phone, begging forgiveness. I was utterly disgusted; it seemed there was no way to balance the books and even revenge wasn't sweet.

MY NEW BOYFRIEND

Fortunately I soon returned to a habit I had picked up briefly and abandoned a few years before.

Heroin was the boyfriend that removed the need for boyfriends. I had done it only sporadically, so it took me a little while to reconnect, but when I remembered how to inject it, and saw the little blossom of blood appear in the syringe like a tiny sea anemone I babbled, "My darling, my darling how could I, I'll never leave you again."

Heroin removes any importance or relevance from social interaction. Imagine such bliss. I was even willing to hang around with other white, pretentious, privileged heroin users to get to the stuff. I was as pretentious as any of them, but I didn't care. Imagine a sensation so powerful it provided freedom from other humans. I visualized nothing more than its embrace for my future.

My death, however, I visualized frequently. I wanted it to be easy. I wanted to die of an accidental overdose or of an illness of my own imagining I called sleeping sickness. Perhaps my eyelids would float downward while I lay on the overstuffed red couch of a monied acquaintance's many-windowed loft under the Manhattan Bridge. The last thing I would see would be the lights of the city across the river, twinkling like stars in an endless polar night.

It wasn't a likely scenario, since the last time I'd been there I'd stolen her grandmother's fur jacket, but I cherished the image nonetheless. I wanted to drift away. At twenty-eight, I had just about had enough. I wanted to vanish into an endless, pearl-gray blizzard.

What would you have thought if you had seen this ill-kempt girl, who dressed like a girl only when she was going to her job as a topless dancer, if you saw her getting drunk in a bar or walking down toward Pitt street at six in the morning with her last ten dollars to buy a bag of heroin? Would you have known she was, in fact, a hideous and cursed aberration? It's a question I asked myself often, the old narcissist's chancre sore: how do others see me?

Probably they saw me as something like this: Loyal girl-friends thought I was a good soul at heart and enjoyed my jokes. Certain boys would always buy the Free Spirit Sans Underwear picture until it came into focus. One pathologically devoted boyfriend stood by me until he tossed me out in a whirling pile of pawn tickets, accusations, and missing money.

Other people couldn't stand me. They said I was just another slumming rich girl, staggering around downtown in the heat of summer nights when I could just as easily be off in East Hampton. They were both right and wrong. If I went up there I would just have to steal the money to come back in and cop. And I'd probably get caught, since I was a terrible thief. Then my family would cut me off, and I didn't have the courage to work without a net.

In fact I was even worse than a rich girl. I was that most useless and helpless of all things: a rich girl with no money whatsoever.

In my early twenties, people who saw me probably thought I

was mainly a loud, cheerful bar-slut, wisecracking and ready to go home with anyone who bought her three or more drinks. This was fairly accurate in its way. Out of politeness, boredom, and a desire to have just one little secret, I must have faked at least a hundred orgasms by the time I reached my mid-twenties.

After I switched to opiates full time, around the age of twenty-five, I probably just blended in with the other desperate, street-ignorant white girls looking for a fix and trying to get up the courage to turn a trick.

THE PROPHET

During this time, however, there were always men. They ruled my world. Skinny boys who dealt smack had their brief moment of power over me when I went down to cop from them. I depended entirely on their generosity of spirit not to beat me up or just sell me baby laxative. Then they went back to their real world where, no matter how loudly they talked, they had no power at all, and usually ended up in prison somewhere getting fucked up the ass. I hoped they remembered me when they were bending over for Bubba, and it helped them get through another night. *That white girl was trembling,* they might remember, and take some comfort from it. Getting fucked up the ass, as a matter of fact, was a sort of symbol of the latter part of my using time, a red thread of its own kind.

Some men liked to give me advice.

One night I drifted into a bar on First and Eleventh, ghostly with the blank-faced cravenness of a girl who's looking for ten dollars from someone. An older man—a guy named Israel who

worked as a bar-back, walked up to me—his eyes brown and furious, the orange bottle of methadone tucked safely in his breast pocket. He made a sort of living for himself acting like a Scary Negro titillating the white bar patrons in various downtown dives. I told him once he was so lame they must have kicked him out of Harlem and sent him downtown to scare the white children. His eyes, for a microsecond, had flashed something like hurt, but he laughed anyway.

That night, however, he was not in a joking mood, and he must have seen the look in my eye and known exactly what I was up to, because he shambled right over into my face and, angry and sweet, began to testify: "You had better STOP that SHIT. You don't know THE STREET. They will eat you alive. You think you're going to get away with THAT SHIT? Do you know what's going to happen to you? You're going to get FUCKED UP THE ASS. Let me tell you something before you let some man fuck you up the ass: You make sure he LOVES YOU."

If I hadn't already been so dope-sick, this speech might have really unnerved me because, as it happened, I was having sex sometimes with a Yemenite grocer named Ahmed in exchange for a few bags of heroin or the occasional fifty dollars. Sometimes less. He would steer me secretly through the streets past his ubiquitous brothers and cousins whom he didn't want to meet up with while he was drinking beer out of a paper bag, never even mind the pasty-faced American whore he had on his arm. After a furtive darting walk we would check into a hotel on St. Mark's Place where I would get to fix before he would engage in his favorite activity, which was—surprise— fucking me up the ass.

I didn't know whether Israel was psychic, whether this was just one of the things he said to people over and over again, or whether he'd been gossiping about me with a group of local grocers. It seemed unlikely; I wasn't even sure he knew what my name was. Still, there was something about a man named Israel telling me not to get fucked up the ass when I *was* in fact getting fucked up the ass by a Muslim grocer, and here I was, a Jewish girl. I was by no means a Zionist, but there was something in the whole thing that smacked of utter defeat for any kind of meaningful cultural exchange between our peoples.

Not that I really cared: that night, all I really cared about was getting ten dollars.

WISE COUNSEL

A short while after my twenty-seventh birthday, my boyfriend kicked me out of his apartment. My parents followed suit and kicked me out of theirs. Friends were not even opening their doors, preferring to stick their heads out of their windows and tell me to come back when I had my shit together. I spent a few nights sleeping on the Staten Island Ferry with enough dope in my veins to make it almost pleasant. The usual ugly peccadilloes ensued, however. I was robbed of the ten dollars it had taken me four intense, sweating hours to make, and I had to admit that Israel had been right. The world was too much for me.

I told my parents, who were for some reason shocked and amazed, that I was a drug addict. They had thought I was simply a thief, and not a very good one.

I didn't tell them that I had no intention of abandoning my best boyfriend, the relentless pimp-slapping love of my

life; I only wanted to get well enough so that I could go back to him in better shape.

So I made another crash landing, through the financial grace of my parents, this time into a treatment center smack in the middle of a lake-splotched, mosquito-buzzing Minnesota summer. By this point, I had completely ceased to think of men as human. They were functions that could either confer on me the popularity, Glamour, and status that I so dearly needed, or withhold it. And even more relevant at that time, they could either facilitate my getting high or they could interfere with it, getting high having replaced the need for social anything-at-all.

On the plane ride out here, the only thing I found to read was a copy of *Frankenstein*, which I'd last seen in ninth grade. It took on a whole new resonance. In fact, if I hadn't been so narcotized, the hair on the back of my head would have prickled with empathy. Flickering pictures invaded my thoughts: me and the monster, large and ungainly, living in "the wilds of South America," loping over savannas the color of sunscorched wheat. There didn't need to be drugs there, we were already high. We were drugs. Me and the monster with the face that looked like mine, suffused with the beauty of death.

In the treatment center I had a golden opportunity to gather people's disgust. The temptation to act badly dangled before me like an irradiated apple, emitting a sick and luminous glow. I wanted to pluck it, to throw things, to curse, to mangle their Minnesotan Twelve-Step homilies with my own dabblings in Nietzsche and Lacan.

Every day the first thing I saw was a poster of a round-eyed Walter Keane waif looking heavenward and declaring, "I know I'm special because God don't make no junk." If I tired of that, there was the poster of hundreds of ladybugs massed together over the words "So, you think you're special." It was too easy a target for my contempt, too obvious.

Still, I wanted very much to belabor the fact that I was more educated than the round and smiling yellow-haired nurses who had taken up a collection of old clothes for me, as I had none but the ones on my back, and even those didn't fit anymore since I was starting to get fat—these women who had been so inexcusably kind. Women's kindness, women's weakness.

I didn't do it, however. Within the best of my abilities, I complied. I was, in fact, what they called "compliant," which was not an entirely positive term. What I was doing, and they knew it, was complying through fear. I had gotten the last dime I ever would out of my parents, and the limits of my coping skills had already become obvious. I didn't want to be homeless. I was frightened of homelessness more severely than I'd been frightened of anything in my life. I still wanted to die, but I wanted to die someplace comfortable, for heaven's sake.

My tenure at the treatment center depended, for the most part, on convincing my CD (chemical dependency) counselor, an ex-biker named Haakon with a seventies bar-band goatee, that I was changing, and so I tried to change my outward behavior, to develop some sort of effectual table manners.

Since Haakon had so much power over my fate, I developed an enormous attraction for him, with the predictable attendant desire to make him hate me.

One day he called me into his office and had me sit down. "I want to tell you something I've noticed," he said, blinking at me with a pair of mahogany-brown eyes. "When I walk through the common room I notice that you are aware of my presence, even if you're reading a magazine or some material, even if you don't look up at me. And so I'm aware of your being aware of my presence."

"Well it's a women's unit and you're the only man in it so maybe I notice that," I said. I was too tired and scared to say anything else, like "That's either because you want to fuck me or you know that I want to fuck you"; I couldn't take the chance of being kicked out. I didn't want to go to a women's shelter in downtown St. Paul or Minneapolis with winter coming on. Things there were very, very comfortable.

When I graduated to a halfway house, Haakon hugged me good-bye. "I love you," he said softly into my ear. It didn't mean anything; they loved everybody there. The "fellowship" was full of unconditional love handed out to all and sundry without question. After four months of intensive work on all twelve steps, I was off to a halfway house. Doing cleanup in the administrator's office, I chanced to see Haakon's report on me, in which he characterized me as compliant, with a dual diagnosis of chemical dependency and chronic depression. I snorted unpleasantly to myself: *"Ya think?"*

Sometime later, in the eddies of information that trickled from the treatment center to the halfway house, I picked up an unconfirmed rumor that he'd been fired for forming inappropriate exclusive relationships. I guess I missed my big chance.

Finally my condition was stabilized by an antidepressant that made me incredibly sleepy. I'd never slept so well. It was handed out to me every morning by a young man studying for the ministry who took the tech job to put himself through theology school. Every morning I held out my hand and he'd drop three red pills of Sinequan into it.

He was, in fact, a little frightened of me, so I treated him with extreme politeness. I wanted to get him to trust me, so I would be in a position to hurt his feelings. I fantasized about hurting people's feelings. Not that I ever would, when it came down to it, do such a thing. The thought of hurting anyone made me sick to my stomach with shame—reminding me of the phonecall to that hollow-eyed electrician, praying I hadn't made him feel the way I now felt all the time. As Haakon had told me the day before I left for the halfway house, "You could never get tough. You've never had the freedom to toss your moral compass. Basically you're still a little girl." I swore if I was ever given another chance I would overcome this defect. No moral compass would disorient me and swerve me off the path to getting high.

The halfway house was in International Falls, the place at the very top of Minnesota with the coldest weather in the continental United States. I was troping toward the arctic, drifting northward. This made sense to me since it was in the arctic reaches that Frankenstein and his monster had their final showdown, having chased each other literally to the ends of the earth. In the Monster's last scene, he sets out toward his death on an ice floe, "swallowed by darkness and distance." I wanted to meet him there.

CANCEL THE WEDDING

Soon after I got my first outside job, I was struck with a case of pneumonia. All of a sudden I was in the hospital with a fever of 106, deliriously scripting a last scene to end the movie in which I seemed to be stuck.

The Monster had been heading toward his own funeral pyre when we last saw him, swallowed by distance and darkness, but his actual death had never been confirmed. I would wait patiently at a weather station somewhere up around the mythical Northwest Passage for him to appear. Together we would live in peace, untortured by a world we wished would love us, but, because of our intrinsic repugnance, never would. The credits rolled over a shot of our skeletons, collapsed in a heart-shaped pile, slowly disappearing under the blowing snowdrifts.

I thought happily about our simple, gentle life, an almost wordless life, punctuated by soothing routines. I would rub udder balm daily on his coarse stretched skin, which tended to dry out in cold weather, and we would read aloud from *The Sorrows of Young Werther,* a book I knew to be one of his favorites. Every time my body was racked by chills and shuddering, I felt myself lifted up in the cold arms of my beloved. I felt his lovely dead breath soothe my fevered face.

A strict regimen of IV penicillin soon put a stop to the pneumonia and had me perky enough to sign for a blood test. The doctor came in and sat by my bed with the results, but I wouldn't let him give them to me. "Get me a woman doctor," I said. "I think delivering this information is a genderless task." I grabbed his collar, still slightly feverish and weak: "Nothing is genderless."

He left and a woman doctor came in to give me the results of my test, which were exactly the same as if the male doctor had given them to me.

The acronyms came marching back. The low CVC along with a CD diagnosis had necessitated the test, which confirmed the presence of HIV. Not a guarantee of full blown AIDS, this condition could apparently be managed with a daily regimen of AZT, DDC, DDI, and a host of other initialed capsules. If I managed it with discipline, there was no reason I could not live a long (in relative terms) and productive (though not reproductive) life. "AIDS," she said earnestly, "is no longer a death sentence."

My disappointment was immense.

Images of perishing prettily on a morphine drip with family and friends in nonjudgmental attendance had been dancing in my head. "Let her have as much morphine, Fentanyl, and pharmaceutical cocaine as she wants. Bring on the Brompton cocktail. She's dying for heaven's sake, what's the worst that could happen, she gets a habit?" I would be softly swallowed into darkness and distance. But this paradise was denied me.

On the bright side, I did manage to snatch a brand new acronym out of the proceedings. My T-count was low enough to qualify me as a PWA, (stands for Person With Aids), which, while not quite as Glamorous and tragic as being a POW, had a shiny, grant-getting gleam about it.

Shortly afterward I received a visit from a health service worker for the DHS who asked me if I'd like to make a list of people to notify. People I'd shared needles with, for instance. I would have if I'd known any of their last names. I hadn't been sexually unsafe with anyone but Ahmed, who, despite my

repeated suggestions and exhortations on the subject of sexual sanity, had refused to wear a condom. He'd given me a tenacious case of anal warts, but what I might have given him was worse. I didn't know his last name and certainly not his phone number, and besides, it served him right for fucking me up the ass at what were ridiculously discount rates. His brothers would probably just kill him on the spot anyway, if they found out. I wished the idea of it gave me more pleasure than it did, but it mostly just bored me to think about it.

The night before I was set to be released from the halfway house I counted up my stash. My politeness having lulled him into complacency, I began to confuse the theology student tech with eye contact and direct questions, both considered rude and outlandish in this part of the country. While he was busy searching his lukewarm social arsenal for appropriate responses, I had managed to sequester a month's worth of Sinequan. I was ready for sleep, to be cradled in a white whirling blanket of snow; my sweet, sad monster was waiting for me.

My plan had put me in a good mood and I was the life of the party all evening in the smoking lounge. Everyone said they were going to miss me. My lounge act was a hit, and I had sucked up every bit of it, even singing a little song along with Guy, an itinerant guitar player with a cough-syrup addiction.

Later, I lay in my bed with the pills in my hands and a cup of water on the bedside table. It was dark and the radio was on softly. As I took my first gulp a staticky voice said something I picked out of the low chatter. "We'll be back after this

word from Ovalteen—the clothing store for irregularly shaped adolescents."

For a hovering nanosecond, I couldn't put any sense to these sounds, but then the overwhelming awfulness of the pun sunk into my head, and I exploded with laughter. It projected from my stomach with so much force that the pills I had been swallowing came flying out of my nose, landing on the pulp-wood nightstand in a powdery wet clump.

So much for a cold and pristine vision of eternity. I should have known—having always hated any kind of coolness—that any attempt on my part to merge into oceanic oneness with the eternal would end in what young children generally call a "noser."

And that was the thread I'd overlooked. I hadn't seen it because it was woven so tightly into my fabric—the punchline. At certain times, the punchline assured that you could end up laughing so hard the food you were shoveling into your mouth at some sticky formica counter would come flying right out of your nose and into the face of all the high-cheekboned affectless demons in the universe. They could control your fate, but not your ability to get a joke.

Still breathing hard, my stomach sweetly hurting from belly-laughter, I put the rest of the pills aside and picked up my after-care pamphlet. It was all about Stress Indication and Minimization (SIM) and Relapse Prevention Strategies (RPS). Fine then, I'd follow it. I'd wait and see what happened. But certain things had to be dispensed with first.

Bride of Frankenstein: RIP.

5

(FALLING
FRIENDS)

All my friends are falling from the sky. Promises, like filaments, are tangled, and the chutes of distraction won't open; like flaming rocks from outer reaches, they plummet toward the lawn where I stand. All the pretty things they'd woven into nets have gotten up and scuttled away. The fellowships to faded, bronze-glinted asylums; the backroom blow jobs won through the thrilling power of their own confidence and sweet predation; the years-in-the-polishing perfect sentence that never quite reached its grammatical zenith—all are jammed into their packs. They've got no parachutes, no billowing oxygen-infused silk. All they've got now is lead to push them down faster. It's not true about the pound of feathers.

What can I do about it? I refuse to let go. For Christ's sweet sake, have you ever seen a body that's fallen five thousand feet? Splattered entrails are the least of it. So I run back and forth with a net, like a decapitated chicken, or, more to the point, like some kind of idiot.

They fall faster and there are more and more of them. I'm Keystone-copping, running disjointedly at comical speed, arms outstretched, trying to catch the bodies so I can sing them to a gentle sleep with folk music and heart-wrenching minor-key tremolos, but all I hear are huge booming thuds like dinosaurs keeling over, as they crash through the dirt leaving huge gaping craters in my memory.

There is Linda, twirling downward, her long hair writhing in silver tendrils against the cracked porcelain-blue sky with the frantic electric movement of boiling eels. The long coils are snapped bungee cords with nothing to hold down, and it's easy to see how it's gray now, her once-dark hair. Procrastination was her fatal flaw, and now look, she's put it off and put if off and it's too late for her to die young.

And falling through the clouds is the hurtling form of my most noble and unspeakable failure. His face is that of all the beloved men in my world, but he won't ever hit the earth. He is calculating the perfect angle of impact. Without it he would be ashamed to land so he is doomed to fall endlessly, since there is, in fact, no perfect angle of impact or anything else. He's too proud to scream in terror, so his blood pressure just rises, silently, one point for every foot of his descent—a silent, strong, falling object with a BP of twenty-six thousand over ninety.

Robert and Michelle twirl entwined, a shuttlecock of arms and legs and forgotten lists. Scraps of things to do whirl about their falling form like a ticker-tape parade. Buy Ocean Spray Ruby Red, quart not gallon. Get car insurance into mailbox no later than Friday. And so on. As they come screaming toward earth, they've forgotten to even be afraid, not looking down, their eyes locked on each other—you said you would, you said you would—and they sink toward the ground in a blizzard of white paper.

It would seem horrible to have your friends fall all around you, onto an empty field. But even as my upturned helpless face is stung by wind and salt, I refuse to lose perspective. It could be so much worse. They could have just stopped calling.

Shamble-shanked and sparrow-hopping on the balls of his feet, Johnny McDonnell assembled himself in his counselor's office. Although Johnny liked dealing with women behind desks better than with men behind desks, his sense of righteousness was today unassailable. It made no difference to him that the counselor was male and apparently unimpressed with his progress. He had done nothing to be ashamed of—hadn't kissed, hadn't touched, hadn't made a move. With a martyred exhalation of breath through tobacco-stained teeth, he let himself fall into the seat and began reflexively smoothing back his thinning red hair.

"You know the policy on exclusive relationships, Johnny. I don't need to tell you the policy again, am I right?" said Howie, a short man with a mustache and a gimlet-eyed glare. Howie used to play bass and still listened to his band on cassettes in his office. Happy, long-gone days.

Johnny's feet chimed in with the drumming, tapping the carpeted floor with his soft Goodwill running shoes.

"Yeah, but this isn't like that, this isn't anything sexual—this is a friendship. We help each other's programs."

"Do you know how many times I've heard that in my short tenure here? Fifty-six. Fifty-six times. This is the fifty-seventh. Let me ask you something: How important is staying sober to you?"

"It's the only thing that's important at all to me."

"Yet if we ask you to do this one thing, you dig your heels in. Why is that, Johnny, why would that be?"

"You're going to say I'm not letting go of my self-willfulness or whatever."

"Yes. That's what I'm going to say. I'm going to ask you again if you're willing to do whatever it takes."

"Yeah, because if I don't—"

"I don't need to point out that you were willing to do whatever it took to get high for the past twenty years?"

Even though he was sitting across the office from Howie, Johnny was starting to feel as if there were less and less room between them. As if, contrary to fact, Howie were coming right over to him and jabbing a finger in his chest. Johnny squirmed backward in his chair, perhaps trying to move it back through the wall.

"You'd like to hit me now, wouldn't you?" Howie smiled. "It would relieve some of that tension in your shoulders, but there would, of course, be consequences. Here's what I'm asking you: Can you learn to do things differently? Can you start with your reflexes?"

"I'm trying."

"Good. Can you make a commitment not to talk alone with Merry for the rest of your stay here?"

"Yeah, I guess I could. I guess I could do that."

"Ask your Higher Power for help."

A power greater than yourself. Johnny knew it well, that old concept, jolly and amorphous, which they tossed at you when you were so desperate you'd leap at any flimsy scrap, like a starving dog falling on a pork chop. You might not believe in a god, but if you don't believe there's a Power Greater Than Yourself, went the old joke, just stick your finger in a socket.

What amazed Johnny, what kept him in a state of consistent and perpetual bewilderment, was his own inability to learn from his mistakes, which, if he looked at his life objectively, were the only things he had available to learn from. He'd spent so much time walking down halls and into offices of one sort or another that by now he should have learned how to navigate them a little more smoothly. The conversation with Howie was essentially a variation of the same chat he'd had with Chuck, the counselor when he was nine years old: Can you look me in the eye and tell me that if we let you go home this weekend you won't split to Lake Welles? He had looked Chuck right in the eye and sworn, but that weekend at the lake people didn't notice the adorable little redhead Dennis the Menace who was going through their beach bags and removing their wallets. Until he'd gotten "grandiose," as they say in the pamphlets, and bought all his friends a conspicuous amount of corn dogs and purple Slurpees.

Typical of himself, Johnny knew. If he'd been able to wait he wouldn't have been caught, but he had a hard time waiting. In fact, he had to admit, he'd never been able to wait more than two minutes for anything at all.

The halfway house where Johnny was trying to walk the walk was located on a cul-de-sac off West Seventh Street in St. Paul; an old Victorian mansion with turrets and porticoes, it crouched on the gray landscape. It had belonged to the manager of the brewery that still sat near the corner of Stewart and West Seventh. Up the hill on Summit Avenue, a broad and shining boulevard, stood the F. Scott Fitzgerald house: a respectable brownstone, obsequiously tucked among the grander patrician domiciles of long-dead railroad barons. From the top of the hill, a person could look down at West Seventh, but from the halfway house, nobody could see up.

Every morning the clients walked up the road and onto the main thoroughfare to wait for the bus that would take them to their get-well jobs. Discharged into the gray morning light, they trudged along, crossing the railroad tracks in various states of hurry. It was a group that might be called eclectic, samples of humanity from across the cultural spectrum: a Mexican American housewife with five children and a contractor husband in Dallas, addicted to Valium; a brunette stockbroker from Chicago who kept telling people she was there to save her marriage; a Teamster official from Weehawken suffering from the early stages of wet brain; a philosophy major from the Upper West Side of Manhattan whose parents were both rabbis; a California windsurfer who still had anxiety attacks from protracted Xanax withdrawal; and Johnny McDonnell, court-ordered, system-directed, and on probation, probably for the rest of his natural life. This morning, there had been an emergency house meeting—something to do with someone's having a little honesty problem and selling off leftover desserts

from the commissary—so the clients trudging up the road were going to be late for work by five or six minutes if they missed the next bus.

As they turned the corner, they all became aware of a loud, clattering rumble. Sixty boxcars long, the Soo Line train was passing, slowed way down and blocking their way to the other side. The stockbroker looked at her watch and made a series of small exhalations out of her nose. The windsurfer began to shake, and the philosophy major cursed as if he'd just been cut off by one of those notorious New York taxicabs. Johnny, who had not been late one day in the two and a half months he'd been working at Pastry & Co., in the Westerberg Arcade, jumped up on the hitch between the boxcars and hopped out on the other side, just a few feet along from where he'd started.

"It's only going two miles an hour!" he yelled back, cupping his hand around his mouth. As he stood there, bouncing his feet on the frozen ground, the other clients began to appear one by one, taking his lead and jumping the hitch. The stock-broker, smoothing the oversized down coat she constantly complained about having to wear because her husband wouldn't send her good one, was the only one who didn't attempt it. The other clients walked ahead of him, but Johnny rooted himself to the spot until the train finished passing and the stockbroker could cross. Quizzical and pointy-nosed, she walked toward him.

"Personally, I don't care that much if I'm late to this particular job," she said, shuffling ahead of him with her teeth chattering.

Johnny trotted to catch up with her. "You're not going to be late, ma'am, don't worry—the bus comes every seven minutes."

"Well, what the hell am I even doing? It's just an outlet store. God."

There was something about the stockbroker that seemed final and sad to Johnny, something that demanded of him that he make a difference in her morning. Under other circumstances he would have been more attuned to the demand that he steal her earrings and trade them for an eight ball of cocaine, but today, walking beside her, he only wanted to stop her teeth from chattering. "It's a hard row to hoe, but you look good doing it. Sound like a typewriter, though, with your teeth."

As they approached the bus stop, the stockbroker stopped and turned to look at him. Her face peered out of her hood as if framed by a synthetic-fur dandelion, and she laughed.

Johnny was cleaning out the ice cream containers behind the counter at Pastry & Co. when Merry came in on her lunch break. She sat at a table near enough for him to see her, a sad little smile on her face. She looked like Tonya Harding but even prettier, he thought. Her hair was blonde, cut to curl, and she wore her bangs moussed up in a little tuft. He decided he had better clean off the tabletops, since the lunch rush was over. Spray and wipe, spray and wipe, he made his way in circles around the shop until he was standing next to Merry. Without looking at her, while continuing to wipe the blue Formica tabletop, he asked if she'd heard from her husband.

"I heard from his sister. She said he'd called from somewhere in Akron. She spoke to the kids, though, and they were OK."

Merry had large, round, violet-blue eyes, eyes filling at that very moment with tears, which only made them look larger,

rounder, and more violet-blue than usual. Johnny found himself sitting next to her, twirling a finger in the tuft of her bangs,
saying, "I wouldn't worry. With this much shit, there's got to
be a horse somewhere around."

She took his hand and put it on her knee underneath the
table, where no one could see it. Around them swirled a
million events and details in a malevolent whirlpool, so they
held on. The ban on talking alone with Merry, Johnny
decided, applied only when they were in the house, not out
in public.

In the coffee room where the clients gathered after dinner,
before the in-house meeting they were obliged to attend each
evening, the air was frosted with cigarette smoke and dense
with banter. Clients shuttled in and out, filling plastic mugs
with the stale, weak coffee from the percolators, sucking in
quick drags of nicotine, calling out to one another. People sat
their hind parts down hard, at tables decorated with over-
flowing ashtrays and abandoned coffee cups. In and around
these tables Johnny bobbed and weaved, emptying ashtrays,
gathering cups, and dumping them in the sink. This was
the TDA that nobody else wanted, a Therapeutic Duty
Assignment that took up the little free time a client had
between meals and meetings. Everybody in the house agreed
that nobody did this one as well as Johnny, at any rate. He
was a whirlwind, a hurricane, he was Mr. Clean in motion, a
blitz of elbow grease and spray cleaner. Whenever he'd blown
through, the place was spotless. The human traffic continued
in and out with raucous, bustling transience except for one

settled table of three: the stockbroker, the Teamster, and the plump hospice nurse from Kansas who'd recently lost her RN license for unauthorized use of various analgesic substances.

The Teamster was tapping his hand on a blue box containing a Pictionary game, looking first at one, then at another of his tablemates with eyes full of basset-hound hope; he couldn't play himself, as the simple drawing game required hands that didn't tremble, but he would watch other people play and then comment, with strong opinion, on their accuracy or lack thereof. The nurse, after a cursory professional glance at his tremors, got up and brought him a plastic-foam cup full of hot water with an herbal tea bag flowering darkly at the bottom. The stockbroker was asking Johnny questions as he cleaned, and the Teamster and the nurse slowly began to watch him as if he were television.

"It was my birthday," he said, "and I'd partied out of all the coke, but the booze was still making me snarky. So Jandi—my sis—she gets tired of my attitude, and she drops me off in the center of town, about two miles from her house. There was a pharmacy there on the corner, and it's just a tiny town over the South Dakota border, no big deal, and I get in there without any trouble and start sampling the Schedule Fours, the Dilaudid, and things like that."

The nurse, who was still having what she called "pharmaceutical dreams," breathed slowly and heavily, her lips parted and her eyes glazed with shame and excitement.

"How long were you in there?" she asked.

"About twenty minutes. So I'm fooling around, collecting a little pack of pills to take out with me, and I hear the cops out-

side. 'Come out with your hands on your head!' So I say, 'I've got a gun and the first pig that comes in here, I'm going to blow him away.'"

"Did you?" asked the Teamster.

"What?"

"Have a gun."

"Nah. I had this slingshot I used for getting the squirrels in my girlfriend's backyard. Right after I say my piece, I go out, into a coma, bang, on the floor. The cops don't know this, all they know is I'm not answering, so they call out the SWAT team, plus two helicopters from the news station, and they're trying to negotiate, talk me out of there, for six hours, and they're getting no response because I'm stone-solid out. I saw the news later, my friend Doug made a videotape, and there's this gal going, 'The situation is getting more tense as the alleged perpetrator refuses to negotiate,' and you can hear these chopper blades whirling around and there's searchlights swooping around everywhere, but I don't see a thing, because I'm out on the floor."

"The whole time?" the nurse asked.

The stockbroker opened a newspaper and put on a pair of light, gold-rimmed glasses. "Well, as a career option, pharmaceutical burglar is probably not the best thing in the world for you."

"Tell me about it. I've been at it since I was eighteen, and the good times are just about over. I better settle down."

He was talking while rinsing cups, but his gaze was locked on Merry, who'd come in and was sitting across the room with her new best girlfriend, Shana. They were whispering togeth-er, and when Merry looked up, her eyes met his for a lucid,

complicity-drenched moment. He knew he had an under-standing with her that was incomprehensible to anyone else.

On Saturdays, before anyone could have a day off, they had to bring their assignments in to Grief Group. Johnny's group had five people in it, and Howie was the facilitator. The Teamster official from Weehawken had brought in a letter to his third wife and his five children, who lived in four different states.

"Wow," Johnny said. "I guess you're the original daddy rabbit."

The Teamster blinked at him and said, "No shit. Except Bugs Bunny would have made a better father." The windsurfer had brought in a letter to the Pacific Ocean. Some people had made lists of things they'd lost. Johnny hadn't done a list of the things he'd lost, because the list was too short: a couple of friends, a girlfriend, and his motorcycle. And time. Instead, he'd decided to write down the things he hadn't had: a house to stay in longer than six months; a car less than seven years old; a mother after the age of six (killed by a Higher Power); a job for more than twelve weeks; a day without being afraid; a pair of running shoes that someone else hadn't worn first; a girlfriend who wasn't as messed up as he was; a conversation with someone in a store who wasn't afraid he would steal something (because he was always about to steal something); a day when he didn't get angry enough to hit someone; a day when he could sit down for twenty minutes; a good set of speakers for his car stereo.

"You're on the pity pot," said Leonard, one of the other clients. He was a thin man with bulging eyes, who was always confronting people—no nonsense, cruel to be kind, tough love.

Johnny's face turned red and squeezed in on itself like a wet sponge. As if he hadn't heard all that behavior-mod bullshit before. He could, if he wanted, make extremely short work of the skinny dude.

Howie cleared his throat. "This is Grief Group, Leonard, so it's OK to feel grief for yourself here. Johnny, do you believe that some of those are things that you can have by staying sober one day at a time?"

Johnny knew the answer to that one. "Yeah."

"Do you know that if you leave here you'll be violating the terms of your probation?"

"I thought we were talking about grief issues."

"Just a thought."

Back in his room, he saw a letter on his pillow. A letter from Merry, who was making her own kind of list. They would leave in her car. They'd get her kids back. They'd settle in Flint, and she would get him work with her brother, who wasn't speaking to her at the moment, but when he saw how much she'd changed would cut them both a break. She'd go down on Johnny every morning before he went to work and she made breakfast. The kids would learn to call him Daddy. Johnny and she would join the PTA. Her brother was running for city council, and they'd help with his campaign. She knew they could do it. Love conquers all. Love is stronger than dope. Stronger than AA or treatment, too. She really wanted to go down on him. Every morning before breakfast. She needed him. Nobody could ever understand how much.

"Well," said the stockbroker, to whom, trembling, he had brought the note. "You know what amazes me? No matter how messed up and out of control a person gets, there is always someone who will, against all odds, continue to love him. Or her. Except, of course, for me. Since I'm usually in control. Anyway, I read this letter and all I smell is some kind of terror. Didn't you do this before, fall in love in a treatment center? Didn't Merry meet her husband in treatment? Didn't they slide down the chute together?"

"This is different."

"How?"

"My heart tells me."

"I don't mean to be crude, hon, but that is not your heart talking to you."

Johnny hunched a little in his chair. How would she know? He watched her laying down her solitaire cards, peering over her gold-rimmed glasses as if butter wouldn't melt in her mouth, as if she weren't basically here on the very same rap he was.

"Do you know that everybody here likes you?" she asked him suddenly. "Do you know you're a person with considerable people skills?" He just blinked at her, confused, and cracked his knuckles. "My husband says he doesn't want to try again," she went on, "and I can't exactly say that I blame him, in all honesty, so the Teamster and the nurse and I are going in together on a house. It's fairly close to here, and we'll be able to get to meetings easily. Two hundred a month including utilities gets you a room. We all have to be out of here in three weeks, when we get our medallions and head for the real thing. That is, if you can keep your little friend in your trousers until then."

At one in the morning, Johnny, who had always had strange sleeping habits, was sitting in the coffee room sorting piles of napkins to put in the dispensers. After that was done, he drew tattoo designs on the remaining napkins with a red felt-tip pen: birds of prey bursting out of a circle of flames, women with enormous hair and breasts holding machine guns, the Grim Reaper on a Harley-Davidson, a crown of thorns with three small, exquisite drops of blood dripping. The pictures gave him pangs; each image brought an old friend back the way the smell of something brings back an old place, and this was not the least bit pleasant or even voluntary, so he stopped for a while and fixed a cup of instant coffee. Drawing tattoo pictures on napkins wasn't what he saw himself doing that night, anyway. He could, however, clearly picture taking his little friend into Merry's room. The night tech wasn't due to make his next round for another hour, and Merry would be glad to see him. Her roommate would look the other way, and in the dark room Merry would make a space for him, shift over in bed, and let him in under the covers. Of course, with his luck, they'd probably get caught two minutes into whatever sugar-sweet, naughty thing they might be going to do. Then what? Some different halfway house, all men, all just out of Stillwater. Another reentry program. His ears started to burn from the dry heat coming out of the radiator, and he felt exhausted from thinking. He wasn't used to this kind of second-guessing, it was as if the stockbroker's voice were talking in his head. That's what Howie was always telling him to do—shut up and listen. That's where Howie said you found your Higher Power, from being still and opening your ears. Johnny moved his chair against the

wall and tipped it rhythmically. Now he heard nothing but the buzzing of the fluorescent light, which had a particularly strange quality that evening, a rising and falling intonation. In fact, the quiet noise was not coming from the light at all but from the air duct right over his head. All at once, the sound clarified: it was people in their rooms, breathing in their sleep. Johnny wondered who they were—Merry? The stockbroker? The Teamster? Or the windsurfer, dreaming of waves? Johnny had never heard people breathing in their sleep before; either he'd been the first one to pass out hard or he'd stay awake. In fact, he might have thought breathing was something that stopped while you slept. But listening to this, this sound like a brook, it was like having a brand-new windup toy, a new thing to do—listening to people breathe in their sleep.

Sunday morning, Johnny was up early to help at the commissary. His favorite job, he did it faster than anyone else. Got the eggs boiled so he could ladle them out to people who didn't want scrambled, got extra bacon onto the plates of the people he knew best, extra jelly for the Teamster official, who liked to put it right onto his plate and sop it up with a piece of bread. By the time everybody started filing in and clattering past, Johnny had already made and put aside a bowl of cinnamon-sugar for people who wanted it on their toast. Marlena, the lunch lady, looked the other way, laughing when he pinched her cheek. As he was scooping out a dollop of scrambled eggs, he looked up to find Merry's two large, violet-blue headlights trained right on his face. She stood in front of him, shaking slightly but planted firm.

"I want mine poached," she said.

"We're working on poached," Johnny answered. "You'll have to wait."

Saturday, inexorable and comforting, came around again the way it always did, and Johnny brought in this assignment to Grief Group: a letter to his mother.

Dear Mom,
Where are you now—with my Higher Power? Ha ha. My sister, your daughter, Jandi, wrote to tell me she's not sending me any more money because she doesn't want to enable me. She also said she hopes I find my heart's peace. Some friends and I are moving into a house in St. Paul and maybe one of them will drive me to Duluth to put flowers. Maybe not, tho, because I'll probably be too busy to come.
—Your loving son, Johnny

In the afternoon, all the out-of-state clients stayed inside, read their pamphlets, wrote letters, or conducted their intrigues. Johnny, no freeze-baby, went out walking by the Mississippi. He didn't even wear gloves—you didn't wear gloves until it went into the double-digit subzeros—and his blue ski jacket he kept open, the sides of it swinging as he walked. The river was lined by steep banks, wooded trails, and rock ledges with caves inside, burrows where homeless men could crawl in and sleep. Two of them had been found dead there just last month, frozen and curled around their pints of Four Roses. A rose each for your liver, your kidneys,

your spleen, and your heart. His feet took him down the path to the water's edge, accompanying him with the soft slur of leaves under snow. Sometimes when people walked down here they would see a bald eagle. It would startle someone with the muffled thunder of its wings and with its unexpected size, as it launched out of the silver-maple tree at the foot of the riverbank. Johnny wondered what he would do if he saw one. He'd like to bring one down with his slingshot, but he wouldn't be able to show it to anyone if he did. Maybe it would talk to him, the way the Indians said animals talked to them. Not that he had all that much respect for the Indians he'd met—a bunch of drunks who didn't have their shit together any more than he did. Then again, he reflected, you probably didn't run into the cream of anyone's crop in County Detox.

If he saw the eagle, he would run back for the stockbroker and the Teamster, who would never believe you could see something like that this close to downtown St. Paul. They'd call him a scout, a wild-ass country boy, a modern-day Davy Crockett. Down at the edge of the river, he looked around for signs of traps, thin chains leading down into the water with metal cages below them, just right for a muskrat's head. They check in but they don't check out.

As Johnny crouched by a small rock, he was nearly thrown to the ground by a shattering screech. He turned and gaped. It was only a crow, which had suddenly appeared like a jagged shard of black light, with a wingspan over two feet wide. In its claws it clutched a red and white takeout-chicken carton. It flew past Johnny, so close and low that he could see its eyes,

wild and blank. With a muted flapping, it landed in an oak tree a few yards up the bank, where, if he squinted his eagle eyes, he could see its nest.

Johnny stood with his jaw loose, not a jounce or bounce anywhere in his feet, absolutely still. And hushed. Crows were better than eagles, anyway; look how they played the hand they were dealt, eating anything at all, arguing and talking with other crows, proceeding through the day without getting their name on the endangered species list. He decided, by way of greeting, to throw a small rock at it, just to get its attention, to make it say something, to be part of its day. *Hey. Crow. You. Crow.*

The crow wasn't frightened. It flew low, right over his head, and settled in the trees, looking straight at him. They stared at each other, listening to the sound of the wind through the bare branches, which was like the sound of people breathing or someone saying, "hush."

It may be that a million baby billionaires with eyebrow rings have dot-commed reality itself into a digital distillation of everyplace-all-at-once, details zooming and bleeping through saturated orange twilights, and bold fonts and graphics broadcasting their silent blare to the most remote synaptic backwaters, but there is still such a thing as being somewhere physically. There is still somewhere that is only where it is, a place with its own smells of specific food cooking, its particular shafts of light filtering through trees that only grow by a particular bend in that particular river, its banks choked with purple loosestrife, littered with condom wrappers and cotton candy cones.

Even if there is no more corner of Lester and Payne where people step out of the Pizza Shack in the early summer loaded with buckets of fried chicken, not since the Lees bought the place from the Ribisis, it's still necessary, at least, to have a postal address, and to remember it correctly. Boundaries have not yet evaporated to the point where it's no longer necessary to know the name of the state you live in, for God's sake, a fact that the thirty-five-to-forty-year-old female sporting all the visible signs of intoxication always forgets when the police, or the paramedics, remove her from the bus every other weekday morning because she insists on making herself a drunk-and-disorderly

interruption to the peaceful droning coma passengers have a right to expect on their ride to work.

"Pennsylvania," she states incorrectly. "I live in Pennsssyl-vannia," and it's possible, with her wheat-straw hair, ghost-prints of long-gone freckles, delft-blue eyes swollen and blinking, that she actually did. The booze makes her waver and glow like a Vermeer holograph, and she says she's Pennsylvania Dutch.

"The low-rolling, bright-green hills," she says, "the barns red and dark as old men's blood, and the steel mills thundering all night in the city, shooting showers of white-gold sparks. Time like a grinding wheel crushing everyone's excitement to limestone dust by the time we're forty, so all the men and women are as soft as powdered rocks. You don't need to push me, I'm going. I'm going where people know something. Not like you. You don't know how beautiful it is in Pennsylvania on a cold morning in the springtime."

ALL THE MEN ARE CALLED McCABE

Listen, Miss Gloria, you talk so much that it makes me think you're scared of me. Graying hair, a little over the hill for so much bright makeup. Don't be scared, I won't burn down your porch by sitting on it with my evening sixteen-ounce. There's worse ways to end up. You think you know something, but you're just a child. I'm not having any in this life, but if I had a child, I would tell it, "Beware. Run from gentle people. They are innocent and therefore vicious."

I was living in Pittsburgh. "Burg" means "city" in German, and "pit" means a hole in the ground. McCabe said, "Look on the bright side. A pit is also the center of a fruit, hard and inedible, true, but from which luscious plums and peaches can grow if given enough soil, water, and sunlight." "Oh you silly McCabe," I said, fondling his stubbly chin. "No soil here." McCabe, anyway, all he wanted to do was borrow money, drink my beer, and tell me how to put on eyeliner.

I used to have thoughts like that all the time—about innocent people and vicious children. Witty as hell, McCabe used to call me, only he had a different name back then.

All the men in Pittsburgh were named McCabe. I worked in McCabe's bar. I served all McCabe's customers. They were all named McCabe. I used to love him, but he had had me by the shorthairs, you bet. Actually, I didn't give two shits if he was there or not. Not giving two shits put me in control and helped me pay more attention to my personal hygiene and grooming. I plucked my eyebrows every day and I was very pretty for a gal coming round near thirty. Every morning I woke up and felt good. McCabe was always at the corner, where I got my coffee, ready with his cheery, morning small talk.

"Nasty out."

"Yup, raining."

"You want a paper?"

"Nope. Gotta run. Gotta catch my bus. Be late."

"You take care, missy," he'd say, wrinkling up his twinkly old face and giving me a wink.

You might think a can of malt liquor in the morning wouldn't be good for my health, but every day I had lots of energy and I loved to get out of bed; stretch my arms and legs. I'd run, practically, to get to the bar. I'd put my favorite song on the jukebox and start washing glasses so the place would look neat when the customers came in. "Hell," McCabe said, "it makes the boys feel good to come in here and see all that sparkling glass and your pretty face." The customers needed to feel good. They were all out of work. They told the same joke over and over again, but I didn't mind. The real joke was that I made them think it was the first time I'd heard it. The first time I'd heard that joke, though, was years before I could even imagine working in that bar.

I once worked on the other side of the city in an office with high, cathedral windows and dust motes floating in the light, and every day I used to bring home so many books that my arms ached from carrying them. I used to think I knew a thing or two. I used to think I knew enough to know what I didn't know. If I had a child, I would tell it, "Don't think you could ever know how much you don't know. What you don't know goes on forever, like outer space. There are no limits to your lack of knowledge. Anything could happen." For instance, you would never expect that a woman who looked the way I did—carrying so many books with my hair tied back and a wool scarf around my neck—would like to drink whiskey, but I did. I drank by myself so none of my friends would know. Then, one day, as I was turning the corner, I met McCabe. It was like a bad thing in a good package; you can't wait to unwrap it. I had found a drinking partner who thought I was beautiful. I didn't go to work anymore. I didn't read the books I had. I sold them. McCabe and I got drunk and went walking through the city, laughing at the merchandise hung up in the windows like dead ducks. The nice thing about it was that all the shit I'd been carrying around was leaving my head, stroked out of it by McCabe's gentle fingers, his soft soothing hands. I forgot the house where I grew up. I forgot the weight of all those books. I forgot my real name, and most fun of all, I forgot why I was there to begin with. A few months later we were out of money, and McCabe changed into a different person. He told me to call up my parents and ask for money. It came out that McCabe thought that I thought I was better than him, because of all the books.

McCabe called me a dumb bitch and walked to the door. I couldn't let him leave because he was life. He was liquor and the high school dance. Without him I couldn't breathe. I threw myself on his back to make him stay. He turned around and hit the side of my head. White flashed to black and things really floated out of my head, never to return. It was sad, but it was a relief, too.

"I never loved you," McCabe said, and he hit me again.

"Never," and he hit me.

In the hospital I wasn't scared anymore. McCabe came looking for me but there was a social worker who told me not to see him. Which was ridiculous because he was everywhere. He was the doctor, sneaky bastard, trying to break my jaw and my heart. Well, I had a little secret of my own. The woman in my room had been brought in with a knife wound. "It's easy to kill someone with a knife," she told me. "Stick it in and turn it like a key. They'll bleed to death."

If I had a child I would tell it, "Don't flail around, don't put on a show, just stick and turn."

I didn't want to go back home so I got on a bus for Minneapolis, and I'm so glad I did. I run in the morning now. McCabe says it's good for me. He's changed a lot. He doesn't fool me anymore by acting gentle, but he's a lot nicer. He's big and warm in the winter with a big warm stomach. He works at the plant nights, so when he stays with me he sleeps all day, quiet and rumbling. I like him that way best. When we get married, he says, we'll live in an apartment like mine, only bigger and with video screens in every room. He's very nice because he knows I could leave at any moment, and

he never hits me. I've got a surprise for him if he tries that again. Just stick and turn, no problem.

I'm telling you this because you need to stop putting on so much of a show. Listen to me, I'm talking to you now as if you were my very own.

He's the type of man whose name is legion—you see them sitting on barstools on Christmas morning, excusing themselves from their shot of schnapps and mounds of peanut shells to go to a pay-phone. They return to their vinyl-cushioned barstools, the seats giving in with a sort of sighing surrender to the weight of their asses. He got the bike, they say, or the software upgrade, or the new Doom CD, and the bitch actually let him see it instead of making him wait to open it until I mailed off the pound of flesh. He himself doesn't actually say these things, he's too tired, and basically polite, and so he just lets the constant news of the booming economy flashing on the TV behind the bartender's head focus and specify his sense of failure.

When the bartender comes back around to swab up the shells with a damp rag releasing a small cloud of swimming pool smell, he switches his drink to Southern Comfort and Coke, just so he can say "tidings of comfort," even though he knows it's not exactly a great joke.

But it's precisely this that keeps him in the bar. Someone, once, at some point, did not offer comfort when he needed it. Now, he will never ask for it again. And if someone did put their hand on his head, to stroke his hair back, he would brush it away as an intrusion, an irritation, a lie.

ZEMECKI'S CAT

At this time of day, the freshwater stink of the river seeps into the air—an infusion of wet dirt, dead fish, and a faint, cold hint of glacial streams. The season's very first mosquitoes infiltrate the tiniest cracks in the screen door, and he slaps them, leaving meaty red welts on his face. Loneliness keeps him gelled in place, which is a lot like boredom, but even more like inertia. It's not a sharp pain, rather it's more of a slow draining. His phone rings from time to time, and when he answers it he is bright, witty, quick, and nimble. If he can't be he won't pick up.

Every third day or so Zemecki takes out his dick and gives it a slapping, usually when *Baywatch* reruns are on. He used to have a glossy picture book of gorgeous European pornography, given to him by his former roommate, an art student who always wore enormous buckled boots and came from a weird and wealthy family. The pages were splashed with black-and-white sadomasochism. Mean-looking models with zero-affect faces and dark shining lips gamboled coltishly through every carnal act imaginable, including peeing on a coiled noose. Not that he liked that kind of thing, but it was, after he'd tossed the Kleenex

and zipped back up, a lot less humiliating than squirting in the general direction of Pamela Anderson's frightening breasts.

But the book has been in a box in the basement ever since he left Happy Destiny, and he doesn't have the energy to drag it out so *Baywatch* it is: bouncing boobs, flat bellies, declarations of righteousness, and, exactly like the McDonald's around the corner, it does just fine for the money and time. Often he is this close to placing a call to his ex-roomie just to see what was new in the world of adult videos, but Dooley had screwed it up. The roommate, Bobby, had given Zemecki a choice: hang with Dooley or with me. Not both, not after what Dooley had done. Bobby had a sort of sadomasochistic sense of right and wrong himself. Something about names having been called. Zemecki had picked Dooley because Dooley clung like a monkey, and had a monkey's quality of baby-headed, big-eyed pleading, combined with the potential for a really destructive tantrum.

So now Dooley lives across the street from Zemecki, calling him nightly, standing at the window, yelling, "C'mon chicken-shit, I know you're home." Dooley was the kind of person who stunned you with moments of unforgettable sweetness; like the time he'd put his head down on Zemecki's new couch and said, "You only put up with my bullshit because God put you in my life. If you gave up on me, I'd understand and blow my fucking head off with no hard feelings whatsoever, man." There wasn't much chance of that. They both worked at the same place, and Dooley was the only one with a car. In fact, Zemecki had gotten Dooley the job so the two-bus commute wouldn't loom so frozen and implacable on February mornings. He paid instead

with his ears, which are assaulted by entire verbatim passages from the original Constitution, delivered in the Tennessee accent Dooley had never lost in spite of twenty treatments and countless stays at detox centers all over the country.

Aside from guns, which he collected, Dooley liked to collect words. He would find one big one and use it constantly. During his last relapse Dooley had fallen through Zemecki's window, saying, "I want to be sober, but I'm drunk. So OK, there's a dichotomy there."

Things like that tie him to Dooley. Dooley's car to the job they both work at. The little stinking sulfur-spark of fantasy that on one of his relapses Dooley will die and his wealthy, grieving parents will do something nice for the only person who had ever really stuck by their beaming boy-o. Who sticks by Zemecki, anyhow, these days? All the people from his Meeting say call, call if you want to hang out, call if you think you might pick up that next drink, fix, or pill, call if you need anything at all. But Zemecki isn't afraid of relapse. He doesn't have the energy to chase down his drug of choice anymore, and somehow making a phone call would be advertising his friendless state. Besides, when he looks at the phone it seems to gather density, like a small piece of galactic matter that, while only the size of a paperweight, weighs the same as Jupiter. Who could lift that?

But Zemecki is never alone at his apartment, due to the cat his last girlfriend left for him when she left. He'd told her once or twice what a good cat he thought it was, and then, one day, he'd come home to find it crouching under his bed with a red ribbon tied around its neck and a note where the ID collar

should have been saying, "Here. Practice on this."

It's not that he doesn't admit he could use the practice. Love surrounds Zemecki, but seems to avoid him, the way a creek flows around a discarded hub-cap. At work, at home, in his car; he looks around and love chatters and screeches, singing to him on the hot summer boulevards and even in the air-conditioned mall where he sells audio equipment. Even families fighting; screaming, whining, spoiled kids hyperventilating for the one thing they can't have and dissatisfied with what they've got sound like love to Zemecki, or at least connection.

Someone to fight with would be just fine; petty irritations swarming like mosquitoes around and between the both of you—fine. And never mind when people walk by laughing at each other's well-worn habits, finishing each other's sentences, talking inside their own little culture made up of bits of shared viewing: that badger the couple had run into while camping a symbol of anger and stubbornness, so the husband only has to imitate its growl for the wife to giggle and admit she's being inflexible.

But how can anyone breathe, Zemecki wonders, how can anyone breathe at all in this world full of other people only inches away from your face?

When he was just twenty-one, Zemecki had walked into a restaurant twenty miles outside of Cleveland, Ohio, and in the cocktail lounge, a room with a window looking out over two steel mills and the onion dome of an Eastern Orthodox Church, he had danced with a redheaded young woman. There was no one else in the bar, and the late-afternoon light had gilded the church and touched the rivets of the steel mills

with a burnished gold, the color that old painters had used to symbolize eternity. He'd explained this to the woman, who said that her father and mother and all her sisters had gotten married in that very church they were looking out on right then, slow-dancing to "Stairway to Heaven."

"I'll probably spend eternity here," she said.

"In this town?" He reached out to touch her red hair.

"In this bar." And he'd known without asking that she was her family's designated one, the one who would take care of the parents when they grew old, until they grew too old for just her to take care of. Her eyes were unusual—the irises ill-defined as if they were spinning around so quickly that they were blurred. Small-town eyes gone crazy from looking at the same things too long until everything began to lean in a nightmarish fashion, watching one sister after another emerge from the arched doorway of St. Herman's, wanting all the time just to get back to the cool, dark, air-conditioned safety of the cocktail lounge. At twenty-one, Zemecki hadn't thought of that, but instead focused on mapping out the quickest route into her Vidal Sassoons. He can't remember, literally, whether he got there or not, but he must have because he does remember sitting in the same cafe with the same woman eating pancakes and shaking, his bones hollow, clothes smelling like sour sweat and somewhere, from him or her, the odor of barely washed vomit.

Women wore jeans in those days, he recalls, with white stitching on the back pockets. It hypnotized him, as if he'd been a bear staring at white butterflies on a dark blue sky. And now? God alone knew what they were wearing, so many

different styles and fashions communicating bubbliness, irony, an affinity with nature, serious business, poverty, longing for glamour, respectability longing for glamourous poverty. The only thing any of these ensembles had in common was their underlying motto, spelled out in the toss of a scarf or the color of an elegantly low-heeled suede shoe: "Stay Away From Us, Bob Zemecki, You Don't Really Love Us."

On Saturday mornings Zemecki wakes up at 5 AM and plays with Louie for half an hour. He had designed the cat its own personal toy made out of a thin wire with some plastic cigarillo filters tied to the end, which moved like a wounded bird or terrified mouse. Louie couldn't help it, it triggered what the cat-food pamphlet had called the "pounce reflex." He stalked. He hid behind chair legs and carpet sweepers. He jumped in the air like a trout breaking water. Zemecki didn't feel too bad that Louie had been neutered. Male or female, he decided, a cat's balls were in its claws.

At six, Zemecki steps out into the cool, soft day—the elm trees hanging over Whett's Avenue with the gentle massiveness of elephant shadows. The Mexican family that lives behind him has already gone to work, honking cars announcing their ride's arrival at 5 AM. The art students, musicians, and crusties who rent and squat near the old Grain Belt brewery wouldn't wake for hours. They'd sleep—Zemecki winked in silent collusion with the quiet houses of the working people—until the check from home arrived in the mail. But he lets that squirming little poisonous thought float away on the soft currents of air. He's got few cares at this time of day, so he wishes it would

last longer—the dawn, the early freshness.

He pushes a cart full of empty bottles before work. He knows he'll get no more than five dollars, and the entire effort makes him look like what his old counselor would have called "a dweller on the margins," but he goes anyhow, and five dollars three times a month is still fifteen dollars and that's almost two months of electric bills—which leaves a little for his savings account, the nest egg Zemecki feels is destined never to find a nest.

At the recycling plant he knows for certain that he's in the Midwest. They've poured concrete over the space but it's still a prairie by inclination—to the horizon. The sky soars like a violet-blue paperweight over disused smoke stacks, brick warehouses, and the onion domes of more of the same type of stoic, sad orthodox churches. Zemecki, long-time baffled agnostic and lapsed Methodist, feels his heart float upward when he sees their upward-reaching elliptical curves, and the gleam of the bronze, which is so like autumn—golden lockets aging gracefully toward afternoon.

That morning the girl—he'd heard the old man call her Julie—was there by herself. Reflected in her sea-foam green eyes, eyes flecked with Slavic, orthodox bronze, Zemecki could see himself with dispiriting clarity: a large, bearded man in a clip-on tie, a cheap striped shirt, and a blazer with a logo on the breast pocket. Large and stocky, like the dog in the front pen, but not as well-dressed.

"I just open up for Steve before I go to work," she told him. "He's getting to that point where he wants to sleep a little bit later in the mornings."

"You mean old," he said with a grin. She looked at him. His

heart sank. A man would have laughed, or said something about his haircut, but women could stubbornly and all of a sudden refuse to banter: you could never tell when they would lose their sense of humor at the drop of a word.

"Steve's my dad," she said. "He's almost seventy, but I wouldn't call him old. He'd kick your ass any day of the god-damn week." She looked at him evenly. Tomboy, he thought. Daddy's girl. Loves her daddy-o.

How did I get here, he wondered. He had wanted to be an architect and live in a restored mansion in New Orleans, palmet-tos and blood-red blossoms blooming in his garden, an elegant wife with a southern accent who spoke French, who mixed him juleps and helped him plot the takeover of the firm. But he knew all too well how it got from there to here, thirty-six and staring at some little sourpuss, the sun climbing and getting ready to bake the concrete flats into a merciless summer chopping block.

He had been the brightest boy in his high school. Had he asked the cruel whimsy of the creator to make him a chemically dependent drunkard? He had not. Where was his restored old house in the palmetto groves? Why couldn't this pretty Junkyard Julie with breasts like sleeping birds take a goddamn joke?

After work, Zemecki splays out on his couch while the cat runs up, crouches on his chest, and paws at his beard, keeping its eyes on his face. When Zemecki is certain his neighbors outside can't hear him he sings, "Louie, Louie, oh baby; little tabby cat," and adds, "mew, mew, mew, mew, mew, mew." Louie lies down on his chest, looks up at him, and closes his eyes while Zemecki rubs the back of his head with his knuckles. He

purrs, sending a hum through Zemecki's chest, and they both fall asleep on the couch.

At the end of the week, after arguing about the music on the radio in Dooley's car on the way home, Zemecki can seldom stay awake long enough to eat dinner. His knees congeal, his back creaks, his eyes roll up. But it's not the kind of tired that soothes and confirms a body's capacity, like the kind of happy whupped feeling from honest exertion. It reminds him instead of how he felt at the end of the first few days of basic training. Sick-tired and tired-sick. Empty. He had been struck by a using urge on the way home; a bottlecap glinting in a vicious wink on the sidewalk had set it off. He'd wanted to peck it up quick like a sparrow and use it for a cooker. Shoot up. He didn't visualize beyond that. Syringe filling with the little water-blossom of blood. He'd always been a needle freak. But he didn't exactly want to shoot up, rather it felt like the wanting was being done to him, attacking him, pinning his heart to the ground.

Later, in his apartment, he nursed an O'Doule's and rubbed his right side. These days his liver pained him, left over from a long-ago bout of hepatitis he'd barely noticed at the time. Bad life, bad liver, hot summers, cold winters: soundtrack lyrics to his minutes and hours.

Still, he could spend a night out dancing if he counted the drops of his energy. He could, if he saved up for it, step right up to the short little biker girl at the plant, look right past her big old cheekbones and into her thin Ukrainian eyes, and say "Let's go dancing next Saturday." He'd have two weeks to rest and prepare. In the meantime, he decided, he would shave off

his beard. He didn't want her to think he was a biker, and if that was what she really liked, she could go piss up a rope.

On Tuesdays Zemecki goes to work early to go over the upcoming week's security issues with Dooley, whom he'd gotten the job as security guard. It hadn't been difficult; he'd only had to fluff up Dooley's security qualifications the smallest bit. They included a seven-week course in criminology at Minneapolis Community, from which he'd dropped out, and his collection of, and passionate love for, firearms of all descriptions. It was a waste of time anyway, at eight-fifty an hour they'd pretty much hire the first unbalanced individual who was willing to make the drive out to the mall. The only problem was that Dooley sometimes had to come in early and then Zemecki couldn't get a ride.

Zemecki opened the front door to Audio Village without a key, the seductive, airy swoop of metal and rubber letting him know that Dooley had already arrived. But inside the store itself there was silence, broken only by the fluorescent hum that was the subaural soundtrack to Zemecki's working life. No Dooley, but, freezing Zemecki in his tracks, Dooley's pump-action twelve-gauge, which he usually kept in back, was leaning against the customer service counter with the sullen insouciance of an off-duty teenager. Zemecki breathed out through his teeth. Jesus.

He jumped, startled, when Dooley appeared at his elbow carrying another gun in his left hand, a Saturday night special tucked into his waistband.

"What the fuck, Dooley." Zemecki backed up.

"We've got them all coming in," Dooley said, "Crips, Bloods, Whatevers."

"The summit?"

There was a meeting, at the convention center across Wayzata Boulevard—a four-lane commuter highway running by the mall—of gang members from Chicago and Indiana. It was being overseen by local leaders in the African American community and Zemecki was dimly aware of a countdown in the local newspaper. Today must have been the day.

"I just don't want any trouble," said Dooley.

"So you leave a rifle lying around with the door unlocked?"

"They have their gear, we got ours."

Zemecki would've liked to take all the adrenaline the unexpected sight of Dooley's arsenal had pumped into his veins and use it to slam him into the back room and lock him up until the distant and millennial time he comes back to whatever is left of his senses. But he didn't, for two reasons. First, he had learned new ways of resolving conflict and had found, in fact, that they worked better, and with fewer negative consequences, than the old ways.

Secondly, he had to admit that it gave him a kick to tolerate Dooley's madness. As if he were Coach, or Doctor, or Priest or Shrink: someone bemused but sane, who looked kindly from a safe distance at the childish behavior of the less-evolved. Zemecki, a good man who'd seen it all.

"Go put that thing in your fucking locker."

Dooley complied, his face a telegraphed mask of incredulity at Zemecki's foolhardiness. Zemecki sat down to begin the day; his liver already hurt him.

Driving home in Dooley's monster truck, which would be paid off in 2007, Zemecki reluctantly agreed to a stop in a

coffee house, where, Dooley said, there were women who would talk to you. The fact that they might talk to anybody at all just to be polite didn't occur to Dooley. He was probably just delighted not to get a visit from the FBI an hour and a half after he'd chatted up some poor girl, garlanding her ears with the delights of the original Constitution and its implied prerogative to shoot anyone who steps onto your front lawn without an invite, like particularly those punks who call themselves community organizers at that so-called summit. Or how if any of those gangbangers from the projects down the street from where he lived tried doing a little B&E in his apartment they'd find themselves face-to-face with one angry, gun-toting, white boy from Tennessee. But Zemecki was worst-casing it. Dooley generally kept his mouth on a leash in front of women. His girlfriend had even said that Dooley's accent was charming and that she felt sorry for him like you would for a dog that meant well, but was too muddy to be let into the house. She didn't, by the way, let him into her house.

Inside, in a room decorated with the kind of furniture he thought his mother married his father to get away from, Zemecki ordered an iced cappuccino and Dooley, surprisingly, ordered a skinny iced latté. "I avoid fat," he said. No doubt, Zemecki thought, because he had to keep his body ready for the symphony of violence he was anticipating. "Fucking Travis Bickle," he mutters.

"Who?" Zemecki asked.

"The taxi driver in *Taxi Driver*. Say what you want about him, but he saved that little girl." But Zemecki, video-educated

cinemaphile, couldn't find the heart to tell him that the film was actually a warning, because suddenly his sight line was interrupted by the short, mean-eyed girl from the recycling plant. She was small, but she filled the room, absorbing all its light, drawing all the color, irony, and attitude out of the red vinyl stools and bright yellow Formica tables. He groaned with dread and helpless, hopeless longing. First thing he had to do: apologize for the idiotic crack about her old man. Apologize nicely, too, since she had that big rottweiler with her. Lying at her feet, it was working on a hunk of gristly bone, snorffling and growling to itself, and sat up surprisingly fast at Zemecki's approach, eyes full of somnolent, slumberous fury.

"Precious," she snapped, "sit," and Zemecki almost sat. His apology floated out of his mind for a moment, and he asked: "Precious?"

"It was my father's idea," she said, embarrassment shading the sloping planes of her face into something he was sure could be quite gentle under certain circumstances, "he thought it was funny."

"You don't?"

"He's a big male dog. He wouldn't think it was funny if he knew."

"I'm sorry about what I said before."

"It was early. You weren't thinking. I hadn't been awake long enough to have a sense of humor." Then her face blossomed into something bright and soft like a plate of pale rose petals, and she added, "It's like we're already married." She introduced herself, her name was indeed Julie. When Dooley

sat down and got introduced he said, "Hey. Dooley and Julie." It was so bad that after sitting blankly for a second the three of them started to laugh.

Surprisingly, for a man who was getting awfully tired of Pamela Anderson's foamy charms, he didn't call her right away after she gave him her number. Waited a week and a half. Exhaustion was the obstacle. To get to know someone. Then the fucking, always sweet after you survived the first fumble. Then meet their friends, a whole new world to contend with. Then cohabitation, the million little details to deal with, a strange kind of surrender and contentment lurking in every dropped sock and split phone bill.

And then, Zemecki projected outward from the sagging arc of his past, he would be struck by a chord of numbness. Indifference. Irritation at her presence, even. No more fucking and drowsy good-night kisses. He'd start to stay up late reading *Architectural Digest* and drawing blueprints for various public works projects he had developed, invented, and commissioned for himself: glass domes, glittering arboretums, silvery, wind-polished bridges stretching into the distance. First she would be puzzled, then pissed, then she would think she was getting unattractive, and finally she would sleep with an acquaintance as a kind of bridge of her own. Then she would move out. It was too tiring to contemplate doing it all over again.

But Zemecki, his side aching, looked out the window at what he'd gathered to himself in his thirty-seven years, and picked up the phone with one hand. With the other he scooped up Louie and poured the blinking, furry puddle onto

his lap. Having been weaned too soon, he immediately shoved his small cold nose into the crook of Zemecki's elbow and hid his face there, as if afraid to look.

It wasn't that Zemecki was expecting any dramatic results. His goals had necessarily tailored themselves to a tighter fit, but he didn't believe, finally, in the permanence of anything, even his own fucked-upness. Like the book said, *Every Day a New Beginning.* Sappy unless you took it at face value and simply acted accordingly, in a simple manner. No one has to actually have faith to act as if they do, and the results were often surprising.

With that little thought, the blind high-dive artist's prayer, he dialed.

It was after eleven o'clock when Zemecki and Julie reached his door, walking from down the block where she'd parked her car. They stood under the pine tree that almost blocked the entrance to his house, and Zemecki called for Louie, who came trotting up, his round, neutered shape making him look a little like a scampering piglet in the moonlight.

"Wanna come in?" he asked the cat.

Louie brushed against his legs and head-butt his face when he bent down, but then he ran off, the night still full of possibility and the scents of sleeping birds and creeping mice.

Julie said, "How about asking me?" Her face was still flushed from dancing at Lee's Liquor Lounge where she had had two beers and watched him sip tonic & tonic with a lime.

They were sitting on his couch with the window open when they heard Dooley's truck pull up and screech to a halt. Nothing

new in that, but a few minutes later they heard voices.

"You better come down here, you white trash faggot."

"Come on down, you punk-ass motherfucker, before we blow up your fucking house."

He heard Dooley's voice come back, strident and resolved as a trumpet blast, "Let him and me go one-on-one, man-to-man. Fair fight."

"This isn't about a fair fight, this is about getting your ass kicked, motherfucker."

Zemecki peered through his scratchy lace-like curtain. The boys were neighboring punks from the next block. Not gang members. Maybe would-be gang members. They didn't like it when white guys walked down their street. They didn't like it when white guys bicycled down their street, Zemecki knew firsthand. And he imagined they really disliked it when white guys drove down their street blasting Ted Nugent from the stereo because, *Hey, they go around blasting their music and this is still America and it's my right under the Constitution of the United States to drive a vehicle that I own through any public thoroughfare.*

During his last relapse Dooley had gotten his crack money stolen by a prostitute and come down hard on a street he hadn't recognized. Shivering and almost crying, he'd tried to call Zemecki but he hadn't been home so he called his eighty-seven-year-old father collect to tell him he was coming down from coke and didn't know where he was or what to do and it was a bad neighborhood. His father, Dooley related resentfully, had told him to find a bus, and hung up.

Zemecki pulled his head in right when they heard the first

shot and the sound of shattering glass. He pulled Julie to the floor where they lay with blank faces, slack with surprise, too startled to do anything. The shots continued, a rifle's loud bang answered by the voracious, rageful spatter of automatic weapons. Zemecki heard a strange howling sound, a scream that contained too much sorrow for it to come from anything but a dumb animal. Then, a soft, barely heard thud.

The shots ceased, but they sat for a good ten minutes without saying a word, even after they heard the clattering of fleeing footsteps.

Finally Zemecki went outside and walked with military abruptness over to the tree in front of Walter's window where Louie usually sat. He was on his side, lying where he'd fallen. Like a static hieroglyph, frozen in mid-motion, his fur was oddly wet, his eyes open, teeth bared.

Zemecki went back into the house and sat. If Julie reached out to comfort him he wouldn't be able to bear it, like someone touching a newly scraped knee. He curled up to prevent it, saying to himself, *People lose children in this kind of thing. Children. That was a cat.*

"Children die in this kind of thing," he repeated out loud.

"You know, if Precious died, my sister would say that exact same thing." She didn't try to touch him, and for this he was grateful beyond measure. "She'd say there are famines and plagues and genocide and more misery than you could shake a stick at and it's petit bourgeois bullshit to make such a big deal out of a pet. She graduated from the U. And you know what I'd tell her."

"Go piss up a rope?"

"Fucking-A."

Zemecki waited for the familiar disbelief of disaster to soak in. There must be some way to make this not have happened; it had only happened minutes ago. Walk back outside for the two seconds it takes and call the cat in, rattling his keys to sound like the dry rustle of cat food. It worked every time. Louie would come in and sit on the edge of his couch. Amazing, ten minutes gone and you can't get them back. The unbearable facts of time and physics. Unfair. And now he wanted Julie to go away. He wanted. He wanted the cat back. He wanted and couldn't have that fat, blinking, purring cat that looked at him and followed him from room to room as if he were God maybe, or beloved. What if Louie had been expecting him to come out and get him? He wanted. He was nothing but a patch of skinned raw flesh packed with the frozen dirt of wanting. Like anyone with a chancre or a surface cut, he did something to make it hurt worse.

Zemecki, thirty-seven years old last month, moved next to the hard-faced family girl who had the good sense not to touch him. Instead, she talked about the life-drawing class she was taking, about angles and negative space. At his coffee table she began to draw a pair of shoes he'd left on the rug. "If I do this the way it's supposed to be done," she said, "it could take all night."

They continued in silence for a bit—she sketching, he wanting what he couldn't get. The first early mosquitoes were beginning to buzz, and the crickets sang as if trying to drown out the echo of the gunshots. Zemecki's male machinery, always shockingly irrelevant and self-involved, was suggesting that he use his own grief to elicit sympathy and sex. What if he listened to it?

It can't have been made to steer him wrong every time.

Julie, he could see, was older than she looked at first and likely had no time for bullshit. She wasn't really mean, but she wouldn't stick around while he made his endless attempts at decision. A man was what she wanted, and help with the recycling and automotive redistribution business. Family business, family first. Daddy first, even.

She broke the silence. "Your friend Dooley doesn't really care about you," she said. "He means well, but he's kind of an asshole." She was the kind of person who spoke only the tip of her iceberg, letting the thoughts build and float in the water until they were solid.

Without him realizing it, something invisible and gentle, but irresistible, like a tide, was carrying him, and he found himself lying with his big head on her lap, reminding her, he was sure, of Precious in one of his sweeter moments. He could see the outline of her nipples under her shirt when he looked up, which made his heart happy, but his liver start to hurt. Fine, then, he whispered to himself. Exit Dooley. Goodbye Louie, my little best friend. He could feel himself floating upward, like a balloon released at a church fair, rising past the gold dome of the red-brick house of worship where he will take this woman and marry her.

When he sat up and put his arms around her she didn't stop sketching, and he remained in place, his foot cocked on the floor in a way that made his knees shake. "If you give me a photograph," she said, "I'll make a picture of your cat."

9

CUTE IN CAMOUFLAGE

Her hats were made of velvet, satin, spandex, yarn, wool, and silk. They were maroon, forest green, emerald green, episcopal, and royal blue. She made cloches and caps, tomboy beanies, and grown-up lady churchwear. She could work up a hat for you if you were a Loring Park art-chick, a senior citizen who liked to dress up to take the bus downtown, a fund-raiser for women's political caucuses, or a bodacious biker babe. She even made hats with flaps that you could wrap around yourself like a shawl, for nursing mothers who wanted to look sharp sitting in the sun, keeping both their precious babies and the titties they were feeding on discreetly covered, while at the same time trumpeting plush tones of triumph. Millicent Milliner she called herself, although her name was something a little more prosaic, like Linda Klemmer. I forgave her this whimsied affectation, something I'm not usually too quick to forgive, because the woman was a genius.

For one thing, she was the first in her field to recognize that women came with different-sized heads, not just the Edie Sedgwick Acorn-Pixie model. Myself, I have a big ole skull, a

wide brow, and a mane of thick, horsetail-textured hair that curls in wet weather. With my large head, I am like a lion when I sail down Nicollet Avenue in one of those wide-brimmed blue velvet chapeaus, my auburn tresses tumbling presumptuously out from under its perfectly angled brim. Think of the prow of a ship cleaving the bright emerald swells, crossing against the light. I am unstoppable. I snap my fingers, I stride along on long, prancing shanks, and all the boys from eight to eighty want me to be their lovely lady. I don't need them to get to work, though. I've got Millie Wear atop my bumptious bean.

That was the second most important thing about Millicent's work. Her hats imparted an almost helium-filled sense of confidence. Young girls especially liked her caps. In them you could walk around and look at things and what you looked at was more important than how you looked. You could grab a little of that sparkle that was usually reserved for the other gender, you could be a mischief maker, you could be Huck Finn. If you wore one of her hats the question of whether everything you said, thought, felt, tasted, touched, and did was beside the point if nobody wanted to fuck you—all that just disappeared. High school girls wore them into class and raised their arms like swans' necks straight up in the air with the right answer to every question, even if too many right answers meant a prom night sitting home with only your ball-busting good grades and achievement certificates for company. Girls fresh out of college whipped those caps on like Jimmy Olson on his way to a fire when they stepped out the door. Of course they had to whip them off again before they stepped inside the revolving door to go up twenty-eight floors for their job interview—but

the hats left an impression, like a warm hand on their heads, making it possible to look straight into the Teflon-flecked eyes of any human resource administrator in this buffed-up old flour mill of a city.

I spent a lot of time with Millicent, even though she was unassuming and modest about her creations. If there's one quality I hate in a woman, it's modesty. Besides making me, with my trombone mouth, feel vaguely uncouth, I think it's a chickenshit response to the demands of the marketplace, or the universe, not that I can tell them apart. Millie had a store that was a refurbished warminghouse next to the defunct skating rink in Logan Park, and she'd done a job on it. In the window was a great big picture of Mary Tyler Moore throwing her hat into the air, from the famously annoying sit-com from the seventies which was in big ironic comeback mode, but sometimes I think Millicent took Mary more seriously than she let on. Where Mary's Scottish watch cap was supposed to be she would paste a cutout of one of her own creations, which changed weekly. It was the Hat Of The Week.

I sat with her in there on Tuesday mornings watching the snow tumble in tiny white crystals down over the city. We drank hot coffee spiked with cocoa and the other merchants would stop by: the baker from down the street, the tchotchke maker from the tschotchke store, and an attorney who terrified me with her grammatically complete sentences and paragraphed phrases, though she did have a warm face beneath her Scandinavian, sandstone-scrubbed cheekbones. Sometimes Millie's boyfriend would drop by with bolts of material she'd asked him to pick up, but he never stayed long, just long

enough to tell her not to forget to take her vitamins, a euphemism for "don't forget your lithium or you'll give away all your hats and burn down the store for the greater glory of God." Apparently she'd done it before, but you couldn't tell. Aside from being somewhat smoldering behind her modest demeanor, she gave no hint of being manic-depressive, except for her moments of alarmingly quick insight and sudden charm. Like diabetes, she referred to it. Diabetics take insulin. In the same way, people with bipolar disorders took lithium, and alcoholics went to AA. Diabetes is the all-purpose analogy in my culture. Everybody has some form of it that needs to be tended on a maintenance basis. No one is ever cured, no one gets all the way well.

While we drank our coffee Millie was making a thick woolen hat with earflaps for her old Spanish teacher, a liberation theology nun who was on her way to Peru. High up in the altiplano she was going to a small vicuna herding village twenty miles from the nearest asphalt road, to teach math and first aid. Millie wanted the hat to be warm, but not itchy. Someone suggested using vicuna wool itself, since it was supposed to be incredibly soft, but Millie nixed it as too expensive, and besides, Marise, the nun, would have all the vicuna wool she needed once she got there. Millie was working with a picture of a windswept, grubby field high up in the Andes. In the picture the snow was just beginning to melt, revealing patches of soft, light-brown rock and pale, dry tufts of grass. She was making the hat in those colors, not colorful, but camouflaged. Someone pointed out that the natives themselves always wore bright colors in contrast to their environment.

Millie didn't care; her Spanish teacher, she said, was from around here, where you didn't put yourself forward with too much red or yellow.

That was the last time I saw Millie before she stopped taking her medication when her boyfriend ditched her. I couldn't bear to see her new hats, made out of cashmere and mink and costing up to twelve hundred dollars. I didn't want to hear her talk about her orders from Hillary Clinton and Benazir Bhutto, who were going to more than cover the expenses. She developed an elaborate scheme for world domination through hats. She was sure there was a reason that milliner and millennium sounded so similar—a great change was coming, she told people who met her, and she was its avatar. Her face was radiant with holy belief, and so contagious was her visionary joy she actually almost had several sane people convinced to follow her.

In six and a half weeks she accrued twenty-six thousand dollars in debt. An intervention was discussed, calls to relatives made, but it all turned out to be useless. After a week during which nobody had seen her and the shop was closed, her exboyfriend got worried, and the police who broke into her apartment found her hanging from a length of gold-painted rope, the kind she used to decorate Christmas hats. Naturally, most people blamed the boyfriend.

"Love killed her."

"A man's faithlessness killed her."

"Excuse me, manic depression killed her. Lots of people get ditched. They don't all spend twenty thousand dollars on the Rapture and kill themselves."

"God, Glory, could you just shut up once in a while?"

"No."

We bickered like that until we started to cry, creating a makeshift wake in the back of her store. It was autumn by that time, the light coming through the windows in the faded, piercing blue that made you think about vast distances and charcoal-colored smoke rising into the sky. At the funeral we all had been intending to drop one of her hats into the grave with her, but at the last minute we hadn't been able to part with them.

At first it certainly seemed as though we should have, because soon after the funeral, they began to lose whatever it was they had had. First they began to seem slightly too much, slightly outré and marred in their elegance by an affected whimsy we'd never noticed before.

I began to change my hairstyle frequently, dyed it what I thought would be a shimmering chestnut and wound up looking like a middle-aged, female cat that might once have been a tortoiseshell tabby until her coat grew dull from poor nutrition and slothfulness.

I wore one of Millicent's creations to meet my latest love interest for lunch. We dined at a brand new, swanky, nouvelle profesionale cafe near Loring Park, where he dumped me over cranberry salad and offered me a job five minutes later, when the curried acorn squash soup appeared. Instead of placing my cloche at a cocky angle and strutting out into the sunlight, I irritated him for two weeks with tearful, angry phone calls that left me humiliated for months. I took the job, of course, since I was

broke, and started writing radio spots for a discount muffler repair shop that gave out free boxes of sugar-cured pork chops with every second visit. I suffered from severe somatic compliance and for a month my mouth tasted like bacon and Sweet 'N Low while everything around me seemed to smell like burnt rubber. I was wearing one of Millie's little emerald-colored, brushed velvet berets when I went for my weekly visit to the doctor for my HIV maintenance checkup. After a brief examination he told me I had vaginal thrush, or, in lay-girl's terms, the Mother And Father Of All Yeast Infections. Now, not only was my pussy unclean and a possible source of the plague, I could hardly keep from scratching it in public.

There was no end in sight, no pinprick of light, no point in hanging on for more years of financial anxiety and misplaced love letters. I began to forget to take the medication I was prescribed to keep the beast at bay. Other girls, too, had lost faith in their hats. They moaned for shoes they couldn't afford. We bitched about the long winter, how for seven months out of the year even if you could afford the oxblood square-toes with the subtle but devastating platform, you couldn't wear them out anywhere without risking a multiple knee fracture. We stopped meeting. And, in my AA meeting, everyone I knew who had come to Minneapolis to recover, which was everyone I knew, was talking about abandoning AA, saying that their lives were more complicated than anything twelve simple steps could cover, no matter how many times they were recited, touted, and shoved down their throats.

People I loved began to relapse: Dora went on a three-week leave of absence and returned with her jaw wired shut. She'd

sold her ninety-dollar blue satin Steeplechase with the paper lilacs foaming over the violet and gray silk brim for a ten-minute crack high and she still got raped by a bunch of dealers in the back of a SuperAmerica parking lot. My friend Seamus's girlfriend had left him just as he was about to take his LSATs, leaving behind only a little white crochet baseball cap that had been one of Millie's last flights of reasonable fancy. I began to watch television late at night, searching for old black-and-white treasures, finding only forty-minute infomercials. Badly, I wanted a drink and some drugs. Out of pure inertia, I kept working and taking my broadcasting class, awaiting a change but expecting nothing but more of the same. I passed my thirty-fourth birthday in bed with a box of three-day-old chocolate croissants, too lazy to even masturbate, since it would have involved getting up and changing the batteries in my vibrator, which, in a moment of whimsy I now regretted, I had named Clinton.

Then, in March, I got a call from one of the women in the hat shop clique, which had disbanded by default two weeks after the funeral. "Look," she said, "look at the paper."

Heroine Credits 'Lucky' Headgear
for Surviving Terrorist Attack:
Will Be Honored Tuesday at St. Ignatia

St. Ignatia's Church on Sixth Avenue NE in Minneapolis will honor one of their own on Tuesday, March 17. Sister Marise, born Madeline Lindstrom, a sister and outreach worker with the order of St. Ignatia, will be celebrated for what Mother Superior and community liaison Sister Theresa

---

describe as "her heroic survival of a terrorist attack and the harrowing ordeal that followed."

The attack occurred on December 4 in the remote Andean village of Eldomarro in Peru, where Sister Marise worked providing vaccinations and basic medical care. Sitting in the comfortable but sparsely furnished visitors' lounge at St. Ignatia's on a still chilly March Monday, Sister Marise described herself as "shocked" when she returned from her morning walk outside the small community to find the plaza overrun by guerrillas armed with machine guns. "We had heard rumors for so long that we didn't pay attention to them anymore."

According to Sister Marise, the guerrillas first identified Elias Mendes, the mayor, and executed him in front of the crowd. Then they stormed the chapel, where five nuns from a local order were taking sanctuary.

"I was standing on a hill just outside of town. There was a light snow cover even in summer, and I was wearing a white shawl and hiding up there so they wouldn't see me, even though I was very close."

Reports from Catholic relief agencies confirm what Sister Marise says she saw next: the nuns were made to kneel in a row and were mowed down by a single burst of machine-gun fire.

"I panicked," says Sister Marise, "just . . . ran." But she believes she must have made some noise in her flight that attracted the guerrillas because they began to pursue her:

"I was sure I was dead. I heard shots, and my hat flew off my head. For some reason I put it back on, because it was

my lucky hat. Then I dove under a snow mound. I could hear them looking for me. They were looking for swells and irregularities in the snow. I realized my hat was sticking out of the drift and I thought, well, so much for the hat being lucky. I heard one of them point to where I was and say 'What's that?" And another one answered him, saying 'That's just a clump of dead grass.' The thing is, [my hat] *did* look just like a tuft of scrub grass. So it turned out to be lucky after all."

Sister Marise recalls hiding in the snow drift for almost half an hour, until the fear of hypothermia drove her from hiding. She made a run for a small, hidden cave where the vicuna sometimes took shelter in the worst weather.

Arriving there, she says she found one mother vicuna and a calf.

"I kept warm by huddling near them, and I drank the mother's milk." After five days, she was rescued.

"It was some survivors from the village. The guerrillas had killed most of them, but a few survived and they came to the cave thinking I might be hiding there. They gave me supplies, but I couldn't stay there. It was too dangerous. They had risked their lives to help me."

Sister Marise fled the mountains, traveling by foot on a two-month trek during which time she was in constant danger, arriving at the American Embassy in Lima on the afternoon of February 10.

Embassy sources say her walk to Lima was more dangerous than Sister Marise knew. "There was an outbreak of terrorist activity right after the new year," says one

attaché. "They were shooting foreigners on sight when they weren't kidnaping them."

According to one assistant to the United States attaché, Sister Marise arrived "looking starved, and suffering the effects of exposure. She's one tough customer, though, she . . .

cont. page 12A

I slammed down the paper. I got on the phone and began to trumpet—I sounded like a crow who had just discovered an open dumpster outside a Kentucky Fried Chicken. My voice was harsh from disuse but it called out joy to the crows. You can't kill a crow so easily, I squawked, certainly not with one pussy-ass little Minneapolis winter.

Our clique reformed, with Sister Marise as our reluctant leader. Oddly, for someone who had seen what she'd seen and been burned raw by the cold, dry winds sweeping down the mountain paths, she cried when she heard about Millie. I didn't care, I just wanted to look at her sipping her Tummy Mint Tea there in Millie's old shop, which she was reopening with a grant from the Order. She was going to make snow boots for the bootless poor.

On the first warm day in April we met for breakfast at the coffee shop across the street from the store. There were still patches of hard, soot-crusted snow everywhere, but sparrows were chirping and the thin spring sun was melting the snow, exposing wheels of baby carriages, cardboard boxes, discarded sneakers. It was going to happen, even though every year I thought it wouldn't. The wind in March would blow down by

the river, chased by the smell of warm, wet dirt. Green buds would spatter over the black branches and the River Road on St. Anthony Main would go gauzy in the dappled sunlight.

We had a huge breakfast, with hollandaise sauce on the eggs, real maple syrup on the pancakes, and fresh orange juice in tall glasses. My new gig didn't start for two weeks, but damn the phone bills, I said, once more my friends, into the breach. We had taken out our hats and cleaned them, even reblocked the floppy ones.

Sister Marise took us across the street to see the new setup inside the shop, but before we entered we stood outside, the seven of us forming a circle. In age, we went from eighteen (Charlotte the Poet) to sixty-seven (Sister Marise's mother, retired health care worker). At a sign from Sister Marise we shouted "Millicent" and threw all our hats in the air. They seemed to hang for a split second against the kid's-book-blue of the sky, like large, jewel-colored birds floating lazily on an afternoon updraft.

GLORY GOES AND GETS SOME

Even if, as a thousand silky-smooth, greasily transitioned lifestyle features tell us, we are spending more time alone, on-line, asleep, or in transit, everyone is very busy forgetting the last time they were lonely. Trust me, however, it happens. It isn't just being a solo act, although that contributes; I know women and men who stand in their backyards, safe in the bosom of their families, at the height of their careers, and stare up into the old reliable silver-maple tree, mentally testing its capacity to hold their weight. There is that loneliness that other people can't alleviate. And then there's that loneliness that they can, which is what I was dealing with when I put the ad in the personals.

I hate the word "horny," redolent as it is of yellowed callouses and pizza-crust bunions, but there you go. Sober for eighteen months, I'd been giving up my will to God and practicing the three Ms—meetings, meditation, masturbation. But no matter the electronic reinforcement, it gets old mashing the little pink button all by your lonesome, night after night. Now here's the dilemma I'm staring at: I Am HIV-

Positive, Who Will Have Sex With Me? If I were a guy it might be different, but carrying around the eve of destruction between my creamy white thighs doesn't exactly make me feel like a sex goddess. But I can't possibly be the only positive heterosexual recovering drug addict in the universe. And of course, as it turned out, I wasn't. As they tell you in treatment, don't wear yourself out with Terminal Uniqueness. Another kitchy-koo catch phrase that turns out, finally, to have the distinctly unsampler-like ring of truth.

The problem was the research. I hate doing it, I hate thinking about doing it, I hate, with every fiber of my being, the process of going to libraries, making phone calls, looking things up, writing them down. Especially on this particular topic, which, to begin with, is so unpleasant as to be downright boring. But there you go, no stick, no carrot, if you get my drift. As a matter of fact, I found what I was looking for with very little trouble, in a magazine called *Positive People,* and I put in my ad:

Female. 35. Hetero. Permanent graduate student. Red hair, green eyes. You: neither sociopath nor systems analyst. Will consider anything in between.

My first meeting was for coffee with a blue-eyed lanky man who told me that being HIV-positive was a small entrance fee to pay to be granted admission into the bosom of Christ. I could see he meant it, because his gaze was a flashing beam that went all the way into the golden distance of final judgment. He had come through his trials with one gleaming

jewel of truth, and that was all he needed, except maybe a partner to walk through the pearly gates with. "Life is a long joke," he told me, and "Heaven is when you finally get it." He was smiling, shining with happiness, bursting out every now and then into relieved laughter, as if he'd just been missed by a truck. "You're sure about that?" I asked him, and he, laughing, held out his hand over the table, as if inviting me to run across a soft-focus meadow toward the horizon. I gave it a friendly squeeze and never called the number he left with me, because I know very well what happens when you run toward the horizon; you get smaller and smaller until you vanish. Besides, what could I offer him except nagging questions, which would be of no use where he was going. I'll always remember his hollowed-out face, however, beautiful and blasted with grace.

Was I discouraged? Of course I was discouraged, I was born somewhat discouraged, but in terms of action that's neither here nor there. "Pray as if everything depended on God, Act as if everything depended on you," goes the slogan I picked up either at an AA meeting or in one of the many pamphlets I'm always being offered by the well-meaning souls who infest the Greater Twin Cities area.

The next call I got was from a man named Jake, and he was witty to the point of glibness on the phone, so I thought I'd give him a shot. Over lunch he began to tell me a little bit about himself. While he himself was not HIV-positive, he had no trouble understanding it—with the lifestyle he had once lived, he said, it was a miracle he wasn't. He had picked up *Positive People* because he was looking for a woman who

had explored alternative lifestyles and was comfortable enough with herself to be open about it. He had always, he said, loved my type—brainy girls, maybe Jewish, with wild hair and full lips and notions of freedom. Of course he was married, so we couldn't actually have sexual intercourse, but he would love to come all over my beautiful red hair and round breasts. As long as I had a reasonable sense of perspective. He so clearly meant to humiliate and degrade me that it was all I could do not to fall head over heels in love with him, but my vitamin regimen made me strong, and I left him there midsentence.

There followed an interlude with an AIDS activist named Garrett, a self-proclaimed Professional Person with Aids. He was always zipping back and forth to Washington, at great cost, he said, to his energy level and serenity. He tried to get me involved in a suit against the NIH for excluding women from early drug studies. And here's me just wanting a good honest fuck. I felt very frivolous.

It began to seem to me as if there was simply no hope of finding a little comfort in the world outside my apartment, but just when I had turned my attention elsewhere I stumbled onto an uncut jewel, a human example of the male species who enjoyed the company of women, had green eyes, and could spell "phlegm" if he had to. Answered the ad with great trepidation, feelings of overwhelming shame, and geekiness overridden by the normal human imperatives. But here I am to tell you, I definitely made it worth his while. His name is Stephen, and I, myself, love that name. Not that it changes much in my life to be, as someone said, getting it

regular, but avenues are opening that I thought I'd have to detour. Apparently the man in question feels the same, because after our second night together, he told me he had never thought this was going to be a part of his life again, and he'd answered my ad out of sheer desperation, which, out of all human motivations, is, in my opinion, the only one you can absolutely trust.

Spring is coming, even to this frozen town, and people here are warming up. This morning on my way home from his house I got out of the car and looked down at the Mississippi. The sunlight hit it so it sparkled royal blue and diamond-flecked. All winter long it had been the color of frozen iron and there it was now, just like me, babbling away merrily in the sunshine of early spring.

Please don't take personally the slight vagueness in my mother's welcome when we're standing at the door of their summerhouse after the twenty-four-hour drive, all ready to make our big announcement. She's like an android, hyper-vigilant, programmed to patrol the parameters of the small reality in which she seeks to keep her children safe. Her field of vision is similar to what you see in a RoboCop movie. If we could get a POV shot from behind her eyes we would see a screen with digital readouts appearing in the upper-right-hand corner when you or any other stranger came into her view:

SUBJECT .... Male, 35.

STATUS .... JUDEO-NEGATIVE.

EDUCATION .... IVY LEAGUE NEGATIVE, Positive for 3 Years, Community college.

GENE SCAN .... Alcoholic present in both maternal and paternal lines.

HEALTH .... Symptoms identical to offspring 1: Chemical dependence, Human Immuno-Deficiency Virus.

RECOMMENDATION .... Do NOT interact.

Of course, since she's also quite human, she will welcome you anyway. Besides, she's already failed to protect me from so many things, a Judeo-negative husband with dim prospects regarding financial security is the least of it, as long as he's kind to me, which you are. Just chalk it up to her belief in genetic predestination.

One of her great failures, she believes, was to saddle me with the predisposition to chemical dependence, impulsive behavior, and emotional instability that ran through my biological father's Italian and Irish bloodlines. It wasn't his fault, of course. It was his genes that caused him to leave her for the heiress of a paper products fortune and die of alcohol poisoning on his in-laws' tastefully distressed Moroccan leather couch at the age of thirty-five.

She'd never utter such a thought aloud, of course—the irony of being a Jew and leaning toward a eugenic paradigm couldn't fail to escape her—but when she sees me she sees the folly of her youth: mating with unstable outsiders and reaping the whirlwind of sorrow that I have so often unleashed on her poor heart.

The unpleasant thing is that she may, in this case, be half right. Half of what's wrong with me can possibly be traced to my biological father's family line, not that I've ever met him. The other half—well, once you've got nature out of the way, one is left with nurture, but she did the best she could. Every mother struggles with the conflicting impulse to both raise her young and eat them, and in either case it's love that makes them do it. Your problem is different. You have to think about the life you are taking on when you make this announcement, sign the papers, appear at my side before an official, and actually take a

vow. You are the kind of man who takes a vow seriously, content over sound, that's why I'm taking the vow with you.

So please, think about it before you speak those words in public. One strand of my genetic rope is threaded with drunkenness, manipulation, grand gestures, and train wrecks. I don't mean metaphorical train wrecks, I mean the actual subway disaster that my mother told me occurred on November 1, 1918.

In order for me to tell you this story, you're going to have to listen to me speculate and extrapolate for a bit. The facts are available; after hearing my mother's terse version of events, I found them waiting for me in books on mass transit and in newspaper articles. So imagine I was actually there, inside everybody's heads—instead of trapped in my own—and I'm telling you this as a witness.

On that morning my great-grandfather, Salvatore Giordano, sat down at a tiny pinewood table in the one-and-a-half rooms that made up the cottage he and his wife shared in a small neighborhood in Brooklyn. As small as the house was, it seemed oddly empty, as if something were missing.

In that neigbhorhood, at that time, most of the men were stonecutters, recently immigrated, finding work in the city that, across the river, was rising at a febrile, infernally driven pace. Salvatore himself didn't cut stone because he lacked the manual control and dexterity required to be any kind of artisan. A childhood fever, probably some kind of meningitis, had left his hands with a tremor. They always shook a little, like butterflies floating on a warm spring updraft. But he'd made up for his lack of earning potential with charm. Charm in those days didn't get you much, but it did get him a wife who had

married him in spite of the fact that he was not exactly considered a good prospect with his job as a maintenance man at the Brooklyn Rapid Transit headquarters. Basically he swept up coal and soaped down dusty leaded-glass windows all day. You can still see those kinds of windows on old institutional buildings; they are reinforced with chicken wire, twining inside the glass like an endless double helix. They make everything look like a jail, and they never seem clean.

Salvatore, however, managed to at least keep his hands reasonably free of dirt when he used them to eat his breakfast, but they were trembling more than usual. "It was eight hours. They showed us everything. I'll remember," he assured his wife.

The Brooklyn Rapid Transit Workers Brakemen's Union was on strike. The BRT had cleverly responded to this by moving their unskilled, nonunion laborers into the brakemen's jobs, giving them two four-hour training sessions after they had already completed their normal twelve-hour days. Salvatore had completed them the day before, and that day he was going to drive the Malbone Street line after his regular shift.

That meant he'd already worked two sixteen-hour days, and he was looking at another one. But people then were stronger. They worked until they dropped, until exhaustion overcame them, and they were like oxen, bereft of the power of speech or thought. For thirty years movements and unions had been questioning this method of grinding people into human fertilizer, but Salvatore wasn't the kind of man who saw beyond the smile he could get out of the person in front of him. If he had been sitting right next to Emma Goldman his only thought would have been to compliment her on her hair, since you had

to be kind to old maids and homely women. If he could make a joke walking home from work, before he was too tired to utter a single word, then he was happy. It didn't take much when this day was over, and he assured his wife again that the training was all right. "I'll remember," he repeated.

She said nothing. Perhaps she was wondering if he was too tired to remember anything. Did he even recall, for example, the fact that they had buried their three-year-old daughter the week before? Influenza, which was boiling in the air all over the continent, killing fast and furious, had taken her in one afternoon. Even when Salvatore's eyes were bloodshot and glazed over at the end of the day, he had picked up Agnieza when he came home, thrown her over his shoulder, and walked around the little room saying, "What should we do with this bag of turnips, boil it or bake it in a pie?"

For a week, after the funeral, he hadn't mentioned her name once. He'd even tried to engage the priest in conversation on the way back from the graveyard. His charm had been out of place, met with silence. His wife remembered the silence, the same way she remembered Agnieza crying on the cot because she'd messed herself, a big girl who had used the privy all on her own for almost a year. Her small body hot and dry, red then white then gray. And Salvatore was talking about training sessions. Optimistic. She took away his plate and began to put the breakfast things in the washing pail.

After Salvatore finished his shift at headquarters he walked over to the Malbone Street station. He couldn't cross the avenue right away, since it was clogged with a parade in support of the War. People bore placards decorated with bloody handprints,

bearing the words "THE HUN. HIS MARK. HELP WIPE IT OUT." The print looked solid, like it had been slapped down by a hand that never trembled, even slightly, the way his hands were doing as he bent down to tie the laces on his thin leather shoes. They had been coming undone all day, as if something in him were determined to go wild.

The street was crammed with almost two thousand people, gossiping, singing, joggling babies on their hips. The sounds of Yiddish, Italian, and sharp, rolling Celtic twirled upward in the darkening sky overhead, strands that knit together the Brooklyn accent my stepfather would study American movies to eradicate from his voice thirty years later. Spotting a gap between a Clydesdale-drawn tableau of helmeted German soldiers molesting French peasant women and the blue woolen wave of the 54th Ladies Guild, Salvatore darted to the other side of the street and up the wooden stairway to the elevated platform. His train was waiting for him.

Inside the brakeman's booth Salvatore bent down to tie his laces again. He couldn't tell if they were just worn too smooth with grease and oil, or if his hands were just too tired and shaky to tie them right. He might have straightened up too fast, but when he raised his head to look around, every single item of information he had picked up in the training sessions immediately evaporated. He was unable to attach any names or meanings to the things in front of him. Instead he looked at the collection of indifferent levers, buttons, and gauges, as incomprehensible and vaguely menacing as the tools the doctor had put back in his bag after he told them there was nothing he could do for Agnieza and hustled out the door to see other patients

for whom there was also nothing he could do, but who would at least pay cash up front. The world, it seemed, was full of instruments whose purpose he could not even begin to guess. They were impervious to jokes, to his soft brown eyes, to any attempt at good fellowship. They had no interest in girls too small to be gasping for breath on urine-soaked cots; they were either too sharp or too big. Salvatore wanted to break them.

He stood there, in one of those dazed moments that is only really a second but seems to go on for much longer. He was interrupted by the large round head of Denny O' Farrell, the ticket taker, bobbing in the doorway like a grinning, aggressive balloon.

"Awaiting the resurrection?"

Salvatore shut the door on him, and what happened next is mostly a matter of public record.

The Malbone Street line's six-fifteen train was carrying 160 riders back to the rural villages and homesteads out by Coney Island. Everyone was tired and settling back to either chat or doze on the ride home so at first they didn't notice that the train was picking up too much speed, much too quickly.

They did, however, notice when the cars began careening down the sharp descents on the skeletal bones of the tracks, which, in those early days of mass transit, were sometimes designed almost like roller coasters to follow the grades of the terrain. The cars began to nudge into each other and passengers checked each other's faces for signs of alarm. A moment later, the train lost its speed and seemed to regain its equilibrium, but the placid atmosphere of the ride home was gone. O'Farrell opened the door of the booth, and, apparently reassured,

began taking tickets. The train slowed down exactly as it should as it sunk underground and approached the first stop.

But instead of coming to a halt at the platform, it continued to roll past. The passengers started calling out to whomever was driving this machine to please bring it to a stop.

Inside, Salvatore, who had remembered how to start the train, had forgotten how to stop it. The brake lever needed to be pulled just right, slowly but not too slowly, and too quickly would cause a shrieking lurch. The shaking in his hands was worse now, but he ignored it. If he couldn't find the brake lever right away, he reasoned, he would just keep the train moving slowly and surely until he remembered where it was. It would be dangerous to let the train roll to a stop between stations by letting go of the lever, and besides, it wouldn't be the death of anyone to walk a few blocks.

Some of the passengers, however, did not see things in that light. Realizing another stop was going by, as the train crawled through the station, they began to jump out of the tiny spaces between the cars, even squeezing themselves out of open windows.

Their knees smashed and scraped on the concrete platform below, and one young woman on the way home from her stenography class began to cry quietly as she gathered up her skirts. She was terrified, not of the scorched, abraded pain on her knees and elbows, but of the shame. A good girl would have stayed on the train, no matter what, no matter what. Now that everyone had observed her sluttish desire for safety she knew she'd be punished, just like the unloved soubrette in a music-hall escapade. While she redraped herself, the newsboys stood,

drop-jawed at the sudden rain of random, tumbling limbs and billowy, white knickers. The stenography student noticed one of them looking at her with a cool, appraising gaze, his gaze as gray as the concrete office buildings where she had imagined her future husband was hard at work, doing something hygienic and numerical, waiting only to meet a pretty young stenographer, bright and ready for her first day on the job.

The train gathered speed as it hurtled through the tunnel, and the door of Salvatore's booth locked itself during a lurch. A group of male passengers, led by O'Farrell, crowded around it, hammering with their fists. O'Farrell shouted and his voice cracked in an odd, high-pitched rasp:

Open up, you guinea son-of-a-bitch, before I pound your lousy scab head in for you.

The passengers called out behind O'Farrell, some threatening, some reasonable:

Excuse me? Sir, it's beyond the point now . . . slow it down and let us off . . . If you know what's good for you . . . anywhere, it doesn't have to be a stop. Mister. Sir. Please.

I can't quite picture what happened next. I can't tell you whether it was the exhaustion, his shaking hands, his untied shoelaces, or the name of the three-year-old girl Salvatore Giordano couldn't speak. Maybe he tried to pull the brake, but his hands spasmed. Maybe he tripped on his shoelaces and stumbled into the lever, maybe the word "Agnieza" came leaping out of his throat and startled him. Whatever the reason, they approached an s-curve in the tracks, clearly marked by a sign on the overpass reading NO MORE THAN 11 MPH. Salvatore, my great-grandfather, hit the gas and took it at sixty-five.

Up above, as far as a mile away down Malbone Street, people jumped like startled cats when the explosion came blasting up through the subway grating. Clouds of rust and plaster roiled up and slowly, silently, began to settle. More than one passerby reported thinking that hell had finally opened up beneath the streets.

There was a long moment in which nobody knew what to do next. Finally, someone broke free of their inertia and called the fire department. Calling an ambulance was useless since they were tied up with influenza cases, bringing patients to hospitals and bodies to morgues all over town. Even the fire department had a hard time getting up Malbone, because the parade had ended and the floats were gathered together, blocking their access. When the boys of the 116th finally did make their way underground with shovels, picks, and ropes, one young man actually called out his wife's name, as if he wanted her to wake him up.

In between twisted hunks of metal, the men, who had no way to prepare for a job like this, could make out severed limbs, ownerless, with stumps of bone protruding from glossy red gashes. Their kerosene lamps flashed in sudden circles, spotlighting hanging strips of shredded muscle tissue. This wasn't what bothered them, even when one head lolled back when they moved him, and his brains came slithering in a wet clump out of the back of his skull. They just weren't what we would call *comfortable* with the sound of so many people babbling, crying, praying, and baldly screaming in pain. It took them four hours to separate the dead from the living, by which time many victims had made the transition. In the end, ninety-three bodies in

sheets lay neatly arranged, all in a row, on Malbone street.

You won't find that street anymore; the word Malbone brought up such images of horror that they changed its name to Empire Boulevard, the word "Empire," according to the people who got to name the streets in those peppermint-stick, rag-timey old days, calling up only happy images free of bloody connotations.

They found Denny O'Farrell, sitting by the wreckage, dazed, with only a broken nose. They couldn't find Salvatore anywhere, however, because, while the authorities were busy identifying the corpses, he was wandering the streets of Brooklyn blinking like a kitten, a beneficiary of death's indifference, having been thrown clear of the wreck into a pile of burlap.

His shoes gone God-knows-where, no more shoelaces to tangle him up, Salvatore's feet steered him back to the room he shared with his wife. She had already heard, of course, and came flying out to the street to meet him. Then—according to one of those newspaper reports in which journalists took a lot of license with the term "verbatim account"—he fell to his knees and exclaimed,

"It was All Saints' Day, Maria, the saints must have spared me," at which point she fell on her knees and thanked the Virgin Mary in "profuse Italian."

For the record, my great-grandmother's name wasn't Maria, but Agnes, her people had come from Cork sixty years back, and I doubt very much she spoke profuse Italian.

But if the saints had spared Salvatore, perhaps they did so because his wife was pregnant. Then again, they would have had no idea that the child she was carrying, my biological

grandfather, was going to grow up, abandon the Catholic faith, and marry the daughter of that stenography student who had escaped the train wreck by jumping out the window, thus catching the eye of an enterprising young newsboy who would eventually purchase his own stationary store in Brooklyn. Their daughter was considered a catch, and my grandfather was all too glad to marry into their family, even if it meant converting to their particularly colorless brand of Scotch-Irish Protestantism. He took the money his wife's family had saved for her future and started his own business, which was a good enough thing to do. Unfortunately, he started it in Florida, somehow forgetting to take his young family with him. She stayed in Brooklyn, took a job at the perfume counter at Gimbel's, and raised her son to expect better things. He was a handsome, intelligent boy and she insisted, from the time he was six, that he would grow up to marry a wealthy and beautiful woman. In a pinch, she told him, settle for wealthy.

You can still see it in my mother's face: he never had to settle. But no one is beautiful when they are asking you not to drink so much.

So that's what you're getting into. That, along with the Human Immuno-Deficiency Virus, is what has worked itself into my blood. People who can't say the name of the thing they've lost and hit the gas when they should hit the brakes. Gigolos and drunks, and, what may be a good sign after all, women who are vulgar enough to tumble out of trains at the very last minute.

A is a letter I've always despised, ever since I first saw its red shiny form in my reading primer declaring that "A is for Apple." It looked overly cheerful and full of a very specific but unstated menace. I quickly turned the page to the direct and sincere letter that stood for bumblebee: I found its simple integrity a relief.

Later on, the letter *a* would torment me through its absence. Everyone else in my family brought them home—why didn't I? It was no good trying to explain that I didn't because I couldn't; I was trying and failing. "If you were stupid, it would be one thing," my father would say, "but you're incredibly bright. How can you fail a simple geometry test except by choosing not to study?"

Later on, *a* stood for "addiction." And other things. A snake of a letter, *a* is for "apple." And of course, "appetite." Not to mention the virus that starts with that capital letter. Watch how it burned itself deeper and deeper into my chest, sometimes disguising itself as something good. But that's often the way.

For example, when the cocktail—a miracle combination of microscopic wedges to jam in the tiny niches of our blood

cells in order to keep the virus from attaching to them like a malevolent jigsaw puzzle—came around, my husband and I began to take it thinking it wouldn't work any better or worse than anything else. But it did. It worked so well his Other Issues began to surface. Before that, we had lived in a series of simple moments and instant scenarios.

The day we got married, light poured in on us in an actual shaft, illuminating us as we took our vows. His mother, a descendant of German cabinetmakers and Massachusetts Puritans, blinked vaguely and said how *different* the ceremony had been. Stephen made himself hug her, even though, truth be told, he could never find it in his heart to like her very much. She patted the arm he threw around her shoulders and slowly pushed him away, moving toward the bowl of nonalcoholic punch, a condition she was surreptitiously correcting with a tiny silver flask all of us pretended not to see. A woman whose tendency not to speak about things made her literally hard to see, as if she were wavering out of focus, she was the perfect crypto-alkie. She spent the weekend with us, sitting in the chair by the bay window reading soft-core romance novels, one after the other, consuming them like chocolates. "God," Stephen joked, "that's our best armchair, we should put down some newspaper."

I didn't care. I'd finally arrived at a place I had never even seen in my dreams: a sunlit lagoon, where water gaily sailed in bright blue creeks down to a wide and shining beach. Now, I thought, the painful part is over, I just have to live.

Never assume that the painful part is over.

Five years later when the cocktails came around, workers were tearing up the street outside our apartment before laying down a new highway to Pleasant Springs, a development that had grown to the point where it had enough influence to politely request that the city build it its own driveway, so none of its residents would ever again have to sit next to the poor people on the bus. Who could blame them? The poor were not grateful for the city services. They tended to be loud, drunk, fat, schizophrenic, and sometimes they weren't white. More and more they didn't even speak English, or Ebonics, but Spanish, or some kind of East Asian language, and in addition to talking too loudly, they often smelled of highly spiced food.

On the day I'm thinking of, I couldn't eat highly spiced food or anything else. I had been in perfect physical health—setting aside my low T-cell count—feeling absolutely fine, going to a health club three times a week. Then I was given the cocktail as part of my ongoing struggle to murder the virus once and for all, and for the first time in eight years I thought I was going to die. I felt like I'd ingested a test tube full of radioactive plutonium-laced mercury. I spent my day splashing the bathroom walls with my vomit, with a metallic numbness around my mouth and a vile taste inside it. Nausea and vertigo made it impossible to walk across the floor without help. The sound of the jackhammers smashing the asphalt outside didn't help. Stephen, who was on a slightly different version of the same cocktail and doing fine with it, came into the room with the pills in a little paper cup. The sight of them brought on a Pavlovian wrenching reflex. "Please, Glory," he said. I didn't move.

"Damnit. Please."

My reply was drowned out by the jackhammers.

By the time the road was finished, Stephen's viral load was down to an undetectable level. I had been put on a new regimen to which I did not have a violently toxic reaction, but my virus continued to peek out coyly from the blood-work results. Oddly, I was sometimes the more cheerful of the two of us. Being in bouncing, good health made Stephen realize how much he hated his job. I spent the evenings suggesting alternatives, and for each suggestion he had a reason why it was impossible and how there was no way out. One day, after he came home from a meeting where he had been betrayed in every possible manner, he stared out the window at the soundwall that had replaced our view and did not talk while I made suggestion after suggestion. We'd been through it all before anyway: *then get the job you really want,* I'd have to take a course, *then take the course,* there's no money, we're still paying off credit cards and student loans, that's why we're eating ravioli four times a week, there's no money, there's no money, get it through your head, *then borrow the money from your mother, she offered it.* Silence.

I watched Stephen stare out the window at the dark brown soundwall and listened to the oceanic rush of traffic heading out toward Pleasant Springs, thinking about how much I hated it when he was silent. It was tantalizing in a cruel way. He seemed to be all strength—his arms were still thick and curved with muscle from the carpentry he had done in his twenties before his anxiety had gotten so bad that he could only take pills and inject various opiates to prevent his heart

from beating too fast. So the strength I relied on was illusory, so what? It was still massive and permanent as a monument. The most beautiful back, the most beautiful cock, stone-solid, like the rest of him. My husband. I put my arms around his neck and kissed his back. He patted my arm.

"A day without Glory is a day without sunshine," he said.

But he resisted when I tried to tug him into the bedroom.

We had stopped going to AA meetings for about two years. Drifted away. Occasionally we abused the pain and anti-anxiety meds we were prescribed. We decided we needed "therapy." His insurance paid for it. For him only, at first. He had gained weight, this fireplug of a man who I still longed to fuck senseless at every opportunity. The opportunity was presenting itself less and less. "I'm getting old," he said. "There are so many different strains of the virus, I don't want to end up exchanging them." And, "I'm tired. My back hurts." Eventually it was decided that I needed to come into the therapist's office. As part of his therapy, or as a couple's counseling session, wasn't exactly clear.

The therapist's name was Sherman Oates. I wanted to call him Dr. Oates or Mr. Oates but he insisted on Sherman. When he said "Sherman" as if we were friends, I felt that same sense of a hand being suddenly thrust up my skirt I'd felt in a thousand therapists' offices since I was three years old. He wore cable-knit sweaters, oatmeal colored slacks of unbleached cotton, and his office was decorated with Native American artifacts. A copy of *Iron John* was casually tossed atop the clutter of an antique steamer trunk that served as a

coffee table. I refrained from being venomous. Stephen seemed desperate, and God knows I'd been at the point where I'd clutched at homilies tossed out by every kind of New Age nutcake you could possibly imagine. No one knows what might work. Take what you can use, and leave the rest alone. An AA cliche, of course, but compared to some things, AA sounds downright unpretentious and direct.

"We've been exploring Stephen's warrior spirit," Sherman said while I sipped a cup of Blue Mountain Jamaican coffee, which was so delicious it was making me want to be left alone with it. "Mmm-mmm," I mumbled, smacking my lips. Sherman didn't respond to my attempts to ingratiate myself by appreciating his coffee. "We've been talking about how it was his warrior spirit that has all but conquered the virus and restored him to physical health."

I looked at my husband of five years. Could he possibly be that desperate that he had turned into someone who did not find this kind of thing a subject for passing laughter? What did he think I would say in response to something like that?

"I'd like to explore the reasons why we don't fuck anymore."

Sherman smiled, a tiny rosebud of shiny-wet lips barely visible through a mossy dark-blonde mustache. I hurled silent electric bolts at him: Little labia-mouth.

"Stephen, do you want to tell Glory what we have uncovered in respect to sexuality?"

Stephen said nothing.

"Remember that without honesty, there is no way out of darkness," Sherman added.

Stephen breathed out a long sigh.

"Start with your feelings about the virus."

"Glory, this is hard. I need to be honest with you, because I love you."

I sat, unable to speak or move.

"Since I was able to get the viral load down to undetectable levels, I don't understand why you haven't. It seems like a weakness on your part."

"But I'm fine. My health is fine. It's just a number on a printout. Besides, that's not even rational. It's not something I have any control over."

"You do," Stephen started to say before Sherman interrupted.

"Well," said Sherman, "our needs and feelings aren't always rational, and even if they are sometimes dark, we need to look at them."

I continued to sit still, looking at my husband.

"Glory," he continued, "I need to tell you, that since I've been getting my health back—well, you know I've got sexual issues anyway—I've started to see you sometimes as some-how . . . tainted."

I couldn't speak.

Sherman leaned slightly forward and seemed to look at me for the first time in the session. He had that now-we're-getting-somewhere expression on his face.

"How does it make you feel to hear that?"

But I couldn't answer him. All my skin felt ripped off and I had no protection from the air, the molecules of oxygen in the office drumming on my exposed tendons and muscles. I looked around for a coat, a blanket, a pillow, something to cover myself up with or dive under, like in the naked-at-an-

awards-banquet dream, but with physical pain thrown in to let you know you weren't dreaming.

Stephen came over to the couch and hugged me.

"Don't," I said. "Don't touch me."

"I didn't know," Stephen said when we were home. "That was stupid. I never want to hurt you. You're my precious girl."

"I know," I said. "But all that repression you grew up with has a basis in common courtesy. You don't have to be quite so honest."

"It's just that I've been . . . panicked." He was measuring out our medication into the little compartmentalized plastic box he used to keep track of our dosage. He had to do it for both of us, because I would forget. In fact I frequently forgot anyway. That was the weakness in my brain that kept my viral load still detectable. There was no arguing with that. I knew it was just that I forgot, but it must have seemed to everyone else that I was simply choosing not to be disciplined. *If you were stupid, it would be one thing, but you're incredibly bright.* How can you forget to take a simple pill four times a day?

If it had been up to me, I would have taken all the blame right there and then, because, it's true, a lot of it was mine. I was demanding and high-maintenance. But there is a fierce and ugly little animal that lives in the dark cave of my breastbone. It strikes when it's cornered and all it cares about is killing instead of being killed. It doesn't care if it's in the wrong or not.

"Well," I swallowed my pills and continued, my voice bright and reasonable, "at least I understand what Sherman was saying about things being irrational. For example, you have been

the most decent and loving husband 90 percent of the time. You have put up with my days of confusion where the house is a mess and I haven't worked all day. You make sure we have nutritious food and that I take my medications and you have always tried to do the right thing for us and you have always made me feel loved and safe from harm, even when I wasn't feeling well. And yet, six years of good behavior, six years of days and days of being a good man, was all canceled out in one second in that office when you said what you said in the name of being honest. I will never feel the same way about you again. Just that one sentence in an ill-advised moment canceled out years of our life together. Isn't that funny, the selfish, irrational nature of the human heart?"

He sat still.

"Good," I thought, "how does it make you feel to hear that? How does it feel to have your skin ripped off?"

Of course we calmed down. Went back to the daily rounds of small anxieties and obstructions and even some good moments where we made fun of bad websites and television shows and made much of our cat, Clump, singing songs to him and talking in our private language. It takes so many things to build a life with someone and sex is the least important of them all—as Stephen reminded me again and again. But nothing seemed OK, really. We would be happy when he got a job he liked. Or when my job promoted me to a position that utilized my skills. Of course he couldn't get a job he liked, because of course, the money he'd need for the course, and the fact that he wouldn't borrow it from his mother. And I wasn't likely to get promoted

to a position that utilized my skills because there were still days I couldn't go to work because I couldn't get out of bed.

But energy is a strange thing, isn't it? The old good-days-and-bad-days homily. Even though on certain days I didn't have the energy to climb out of bed, on others I was able to climb into it. With someone else. In someone else's little bachelor pad. Someone who was into sex to the degree that he would throw me up against a wall, squeeze on a ribbed condom, and shove his cock into me regardless of my HIV status. I became obsessed. To feel a man's body up against mine, the slow clockwise grind of blue-jeaned crotches, his getting hard. To be aware of my hips and breasts and pussy and mouth—all those little things.

Stephen looked at me and decided not to believe it. But he had to believe in the fact that I'd started drinking. Well, I had to drink, I said to my former AA sponsor. If I didn't drink I would feel too guilty to enjoy the cheating sex I was having. "You're not thinking clearly," she said. "Trying to avoid pain is making you think like a crazy person."

I didn't care what she said. I only knew I had to get fucked.

Finally what I did was stay out all night, downing shots of tequila and watching dirty movies with my source of sex, who was getting a little tired of my intensity and thinking he had better find a nice girl and settle down. I have that effect on men, sometimes, sending them screaming back to the girl next door, a phenomenon which I regard with a mixture of embarrassment and pride. But I can't regard what happened with even the bitter pride of those who take refuge in their own culpability.

With my hands in my pockets to cover up their booze-with-drawal flutter, I walked up the street after leaving the guy's house. I stopped at a convenience store. It was around eleven in the morning. I was standing at the coffee machine when I felt a tap on my shoulder. There was Stephen, a man who could hoist eighty-pound bags of turf over his shoulder like they were toddlers, standing before me. His eyes were wavery with tears. I'd never seen him cry before. What does it take to make a man with that kind of hunkered-down solidity cry? Simple: rip his skin off.

I took the final *a* word to heart. Adultery. I would not let anyone forgive me for it. To be forgiven would be too disgusting. I moved into a studio apartment, on the other side of the Pleasant Springs highway. Same view of a soundwall, but the windows were high, cathedral-style panes that let in the light. I was standing in front of them with the sun on my face when my husband, from whom I'd been separated for almost two years, called.

"I passed. They said they'll have a job for me in September."

"That's fabulous, baby, I'm so glad for you."

He'd asked his mother to lend him the money for the class a month after we separated.

As for myself, I was taking my meds religiously. I never missed a dose.

No one knows exactly when the merciful end of time will finally arrive, but when it does, it's making its first stop at the City Coin Wash & Dri on the corner of Nicollet and 28th. Where else would the end of time pick to enter the universe but at a laundromat on a tumbledown avenue with no trees in a third-tier metropolis like Minneapolis, City We Love? No one will notice it at first because the end of time seeps in like the smell of warm wet earth in March even though the wind still blows and the sky is gray as frozen iron. The end of time-let's-call-it-mercy will seep in through the clouded windows that make up the walls of the Wash & Dri, like dust filtering through shafts of light, a thin dancing ribbon of invisible ink entering a slow-moving river.

And what will happen is simple: The silent breeze of mercy will blow through everything, starting with the wet socks and logo-blasted T-shirts sudsing behind the clear round windows of the washing machines. The squawking children clambering over mountainous piles of dirty clothes will stop to stare, transfixed, their eyes as glossy as the dark gleaming portholes

with things spinning around inside them. Soapsuds begin to twinkle like diamonds in the blackness of the double loaders, but the din continues on a Sunday evening like any Sunday evening, coins jangling out of change machines, as the manager—a grinning woman with straggling mouse-colored hair, hips that roll like ocean liners, and a pale pockmarked face—blares out her friendly Klaxon bellow into the noise: "45 is FREE. Two-minute wait on 18 over here by the extractor."

It's the man with the hockey-helmet hairdo and the homemade identical "Fuck Rice Burners" tattoos running up both his rope-muscled arms who notices it first. He's folding baby clothes, tiny underpants with dinosaurs on them, and striped navy-and-white ladies' work blouses that belong to his wife who is working right now in the office of an industrial park somewhere in the sprawling drone of the outer limits an hour-and-fifteen-minute bus ride away from her husband, her little boy, and their four-room house on Portland Avenue. Pausing in midfold, he catches a glimpse of the manager, large and homely as always in her too-tight stonewashed jeans—and suddenly she is what, for lack of a better word, he's going to call beautiful. Her smile beams, her eyes blaze, and the jangle of keys at her ample waist sounds like the church bells in his hometown of La Crosse, Wisconsin, started chiming all at once.

Aware that he's caught on, she smiles more broadly and lets go of the metal mop bucket she's been pushing since she was born and lets it slide across the tilted linoleum floor, children skittering out of its way like flocks of startled ducklings. Unstoppable, it continues its implacable, magisterial roll past

the two women with burnt-orange hair and high sharp cheek-bones who are folding what looks like all the laundry in the world, bending down to the pile, putting the clothes on the table, and folding as they talk, talking about white women who don't care who sees their panties, waving those nasty things around like searchlights at a supermarket opening. "I wash my lingerie at HOME in the SINK," the one is saying when her mouth drops open as she and her friend look at the table to find their clothes are folded, neat, perfect, and packed as tightly as feathers on the wing of a soft white bird.

All over City Coin the bending and folding and sorting stops while people stand and stare at each other with the same expression on their faces, as if they'd finally gotten the same joke. The three apprentice nail technicians from Lam's Beauty Salon across the parking lot who had been bleaching the table linens unroll their bolts of satiny hair and begin to laugh.

Laughter is how you'll know the merciful end of time has made its first stop, that and the people running outside to tell everyone. All the customers in City Coin scatter down the block, shouting and tumbling, and the street will be left in silence. The store windows will catch the blue evening light and shine like eyes filled with religion.

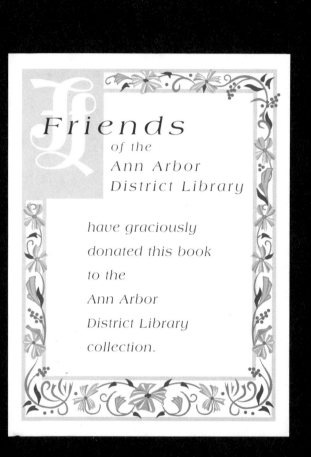

Friends
of the
Ann Arbor
District Library

have graciously
donated this book
to the
Ann Arbor
District Library
collection.